A Sense of Miss Direction

A.G. Aragon

To Adam —
— If it hadn't been for you, I would have never seen Italy with my amazing family & friends.
Thank you so much for supporting my book and for your friendship.
♡ Andee

Grateful acknowledgement is made for permission to reprint an excerpt from the following copyrighted material:

Lyrics from "Relapse" by Prudy Dimas, Copyright © 2013. *Love And How To Live Without It*. All rights reserved. Used by permission.

Lyrics from "Hesitate" and "Fall" by Ray Ortiz, Copyright © 2001. *Candlerise*. All rights reserved. Used by permission.

Lyrics from "Waiting for You" by Ray Ortiz. All rights reserved. Used by permission.

Cover image by Chikiyo Jackson, Copyright © 2015. Imminent Photography LLC. All rights reserved. Used by permission.

Copyright © 2015 A.G. Aragon

All rights reserved.

ISBN-13: 978-1-508-45851-7
ISBN-10: 1-508-45851-0

For my nieces…Raylan, Harper, and Violet.

Never, ever forget what you're worth.

You are the best of all of us.

♪

if i just count the times i lost count of you
i might win the fight in my head

— PRUDY DIMAS,
"Relapse"

CHAPTER ONE

When Anna met Luke for the first time it was at a party for a mutual friend. She had only been back in town for about eight months, but she had been doing a pretty good job of keeping herself busy. That is, when she wasn't obsessing about her ex and breaking down in the middle of a perfectly good day hanging out with her sister. As pathetic as it sounded to Anna when she thought about it now, she had actually spent a lot of time over-analyzing the demise of her relationship with Collen. What woman doesn't over-analyze though? It's as much a part of their DNA as long legs, large breasts, and hair that gets unattractively frizzy when exposed to humidity. Of course, Anna was blessed with only the last of these traits, but as long as she lived in the dry climate of the southwest, she was in good shape. That and the fact that she had a nice ass - she could thank her grandmother's genes for that.

Anna wasn't someone you would call beautiful, but there was definitely something about her that made people think she was attractive. She wasn't tall and lean, but was of average height and somewhat curvy. She had accepted the fact long ago that her stomach would never be perfectly flat, like so many of the women lounging around the pool on a hot summer day. Her jet black hair fell in waves around her ivory colored face, and her dark brown eyes were accentuated by long eyelashes. She wore little makeup – just enough to get the job done. She was just never good at using it, or at the daily facial upkeep that came with the territory of being a woman. She could actually remember the first time her mother sat her down to teach her how to pluck her eyebrows.

"You look like a muppet," her mother said. "You have just one black line underneath your forehead." Her little sister Alyssa thought this was hilarious. Anna sat there mortified as Alyssa walked out of the room laughing with the phone to her ear. "You would never believe what my mom just told my sister!" Anna overheard Alyssa saying. That was definitely not one of those happy picture-perfect family moments. However, Anna got to have her revenge laugh a couple of years later, the day Alyssa over-plucked and ended up looking like a cartoon character with pencil lines where her eyebrows should be.

No, Anna wasn't beautiful, but she was attractive - mostly because of her personality and the way she held herself. Her friend Alex told her once that she could light up a room with her smile and her laugh alone. Anna always thought that was one of the nicest compliments she had ever received, and she knew Alex didn't tell her that just to get her into bed. They had actually been dating for a few months. However, if they hadn't already been sleeping together, she had to admit that line would have definitely worked.

That was a long time ago though. Before Collen. Before she really knew what it meant to fall in love. Before everything came crashing down. Even now though, as she sat listening to the conversation around her, she missed him. She missed the man who broke her heart so badly, Anna knew some of the pieces could never be put back where they once belonged.

She sat watching Luke talk to the small group of people sitting in a circle on the patio. It was a beautiful night. The sky was clear and the stars were easily visible. Anna looked up at the moon. Venus was shining brightly next to it. She took a deep, slow breath in, and as she released it, she felt her heart become lighter.

"*This is why I moved back*," she thought to herself. She felt truly at home here – as though the part of herself she had lost a few months before was slowly reemerging with every leisurely dinner she had with her friends, every orange and red sunset she watched, and every turn she made onto a familiar street as she drove around the city. She loved that she didn't have to think when she went anywhere in Albuquerque. She had lived there so long that her mind could easily wander when she was behind the wheel of her car. This, of course, was an enormous feat because Anna got lost everywhere. It was just the way it was, like the fact that it always rains when you wash your car, or how the one night you're home to watch your favorite TV show, it's a rerun.

She had gotten lost multiple times when she moved to Washington DC with Collen, no thanks to the large number of maps she printed out on the Internet. Since their main purpose had gone unfulfilled, they had simply accumulated under the passenger's seat of her car, slowly forming a small map graveyard. Collen used to tease her for not being able to get anywhere without a GPS or a trail of breadcrumbs leading her back home. Over time, she learned to rely on him to get everywhere. Thinking about it now, Anna realized he had been her beacon in more ways than one.

It was for this reason alone, that Anna had never felt more lost in her life. Only two years ago, she and Collen had packed up their moving van and made the long trek to the east coast. She thought they had been driving towards their future. Who would have known that she would be thrown turbulently off course by Collen's confessions of infidelity? She hated that word – *infidelity*. It sounded so proper, when nothing about it was proper at all. *Screwing around* was a much better phrase and a lot closer to the truth. Yes. Collen had screwed around and she had left. It really was simple. Too simple when she thought about it…so simple it hurt all the time.

She had agreed to come to the party anyway though. Sitting at home just didn't work for her, and Matt and Lila had been nice enough to invite her. It had been the week before, when Anna was hanging out at their house.

"You really should come next weekend Anna," Matt said as he cut a lime into fourths. "It's at Steve's house. He graduated from his Master's program. There's gonna be lots of booze!" he said excitedly with a large grin that was quickly followed by a scowl, as half of a lime rolled off the counter and fell onto the floor. Matt loved calling alcohol booze.

"Matt, you're so lame," Lila replied with a smirk on her face that clearly suggested no matter how lame she accused Matt of being, she loved him.

Anna smiled as she watched Matt do an awkward version of "the robot". Lila giggled at him, obviously charmed by his skills. Anna really had missed them.

"Come Anna! It will be good for you to get out and Steve would love to see you." Lila was pulling on Anna's arm as she said this, as if they were going to go walk over right then and there. Anna had met Steve through Matt and Lila a few years before. They all used to hang out a lot before she started dating Collen.

"Maybe," Anna found herself saying. She definitely loved seeing her friends, but her emotions were all over the place these days, and she couldn't promise that she wouldn't be in the middle of a full-blown pity party when it would be time to go.

"Can I keep you posted?" she asked Lila. Matt was busy pouring a drink that was looking like it contained three-fourths gin and very little tonic. It was going to be a fun night.

"Sure!" Lila replied. "But really think about it. It'll be a good time!"

"There's gonna be booze!" Matt happily repeated as he took a drink from his gin loaded glass. Anna looked at Lila and laughed.

"Weirdo," Lila said looking disdainfully at Matt before planting a kiss on his cheek. He gave Anna a quick wink, as he threw part of a lime at Lila.

So, here she was at Steve's party, listening to Luke tell a

random story about visiting a small town in Mexico. It was before he had learned Spanish, but that hadn't stopped him from jumping on a bus one summer to head down south and explore. The problem was that he had gotten off at the wrong stop in the middle of the night, due to the fact that he had no idea what the bus driver was saying.

"So, I'm standing in the middle of this tiny bus station with no other buildings around," Luke recalled to the group, "And it doesn't take me long to realize that I better make friends with the only little old lady sitting in the place, because I have no idea where I am! Imagine some strange guy looking like me coming up to you, a sweet little Mexican lady, in the middle of the night!" The group instantly broke out in laughter, as did Luke. He shook his head from side to side and was trying to catch his breath long enough to spout out words two at a time and finish his story. Anna liked him. He seemed genuine and there was a kindness in his eyes. He looked at her and broke out a large smile. She smiled back, but then quickly looked down as she felt herself blush. She pretended to fiddle with some cubes of cheese on her plate.

She couldn't help but wonder what the hell she was doing. It had been a long time since Anna had been attracted to anybody. She hadn't even given other men a second thought when she was with Collen. Everything about him fulfilled her to the point where other men weren't even interesting. Yet, here she was smiling at some guy she didn't even know. She blamed it on the drink Matt had given her awhile earlier. Damn vodka.

She looked up from her plate to find that Luke was still smiling at her. Again, she felt herself blush. Okay, enough was enough. She wasn't some sixteen-year-old girl with a crush! She was ten years older than that, recently dumped, and ready to go home. Maybe this party was a bad idea. She quickly got up from her chair, hurled her paper plate into a nearby trash can, and went into the house to find Lila. She spotted her in the living room talking to Steve.

"Hey girlie!" Lila said as Anna walked up. "Having fun?"

"Anna!" Steve said excitedly, as he put his arms around her. "I'm so glad you came! It's been ages since I've seen you! Why the hell did you ever leave in the first place? DC sucks! And why did you ever go with that guy? I couldn't stand him! What a jerkoff!"

"Now you tell me," Anna thought to herself. She sighed heavily and could feel the thoughts in her mind swirling. As wonderfully supportive as her friends had been the past few months, what Steve had just told her wasn't new information. Apparently, most of her friends never had warm, fuzzy feelings about Collen from the beginning – and it seemed they were more than happy to let her know now that he was completely out of the picture.

"Lila, do you think Matt would mind driving me home? I'm not feeling too good." Even as she said it, Anna could feel the lump in her throat forming. She gave Steve an apologetic glance and reached out for Lila's hand.

"What's wrong?" Lila asked. Anna could hear the worry in her voice.

"It's just one of those nights," Anna said sadly. She turned her head and felt her stomach jump. Luke was walking towards them.

"We just got here sweetie," Lila whispered as she moved closer to Anna and squeezed her hand. "Are you sure you want to go?"

Anna thought about how to answer this question as Luke got closer. He was only a few steps away now. "I don't know," she said softly...and the truth was she didn't. All she did know was that she was affected by another man for the first time in almost four years, and it was a strange, if not unsettling, feeling. In some ridiculous way, she almost felt as though she was cheating on Collen.

"*But you're not,*" she told herself. "*You're broken up. He's moved on. Now it's your turn.*"

Luke was standing next to her now. She didn't realize how tall he was until then. He must have been at least six feet. Her heart started beating a little faster now.

Was she ready for this?

"Hey," he said. His voice was low and gentle. He meant to address all three of them, but his eyes were clearly on Anna. They were the most beautiful blue eyes she had ever seen. Anna felt something inside of her relax as his arm softly brushed up against her. For the first time all night, she didn't look away.

"Hi," she heard herself say. Inside she was trembling, but her voice came out smooth and confident. Lila and Steve took that as their cue to leave. They quickly walked away, but not before giving each other a knowing glance.

"I'm Luke," he said to Anna, as he held his hand out to grasp hers. For the first time in months, Anna felt the warmth of a man's touch as she put her hand in his. She felt his fingers tighten around hers for just a second. It felt nice, comfortable, familiar.

"I'm Anna," she said, not letting go of his hand. Luke's smile broadened.

"Well, Anna," he said, "It's wonderful to meet you."

That was all it took for Anna Melone to decide that maybe it wouldn't be such a bad idea to stay at the party after all.

CHAPTER TWO

"Anna! Have you seen my wallet?" Luke yelled out from the living room.

Anna was in the kitchen pouring some coffee in a thermos for him to take to work. It was a typical morning in her small, one bedroom apartment. Regardless of the fact that there was only about 600 square feet surrounding them, Luke was struggling to find the wallet that Anna could clearly see sitting on top of the television set.

"Sweetie, it's on top of the TV," Anna replied, as she walked out of the kitchen and scooped up the wallet. She handed it and the thermos to Luke. He smiled happily and gave her a quick kiss.

"Thanks babe! What would I do without you?" Luke said as he put on his jacket and headed towards the door. "See you tonight! Love you!"

As Anna heard the door close, she looked over to the kitchen table. Luke's computer bag was lying on top of it. A small smile came over her face. "One…two…three…," she slowly counted to herself. On four, she heard someone bounding up the steps to her front door. A couple of seconds later, Luke came bursting into the room. "Anna! Have you seen my…" he didn't even have to finish his sentence. Anna was standing in front of him holding the computer bag in her outstretched arms.

"Looking for this?" she said in a toying voice. Luke took the bag out of her hands and dropped it on the floor. "No," he said. "I was looking for you." He kissed her softly on the forehead and then on the lips. She felt herself melt into him, enjoying the moment, breathing in the smell of him. He always smelled good to her, even though he didn't wear cologne…it was just a simple combination of laundry detergent and bar soap – but all too quickly he was pulling away. They needed him at work, and she had learned to accept that he could quickly forget her when preoccupied with the other joys of his day.

"I better go! I'm gonna be late! Love you!" His voice was full of energy, as was the rest of him, as he scooped up the bag and ran out the door, which had been left wide open after his initial reappearance.

Luke loved his job and usually tried to get in early. He was a middle school counselor – a job that most people would find almost too challenging. Luke appreciated and admired the students that grudgingly visited him every day though. He once told Anna that they made him appreciate life more, not because they struggled and he didn't, but because they struggled and still had the courage to come into his office. "A lot of times, people don't ask for help Anna," Luke told her once as they were lying in bed next to each other. Her head was resting on his chest, and she could feel his heart beating softly underneath her hand. "Most of the time, they try and pretend everything's fine, while slowly passing their anger and insecurities on to everyone else around them."

Anna remembered this conversation because it was about three months after they had started dating, and it made her see just how different Luke was from other men she had dated. She realized at that moment that her attraction to him was no coincidence. He was put in her life to help her heal. Like the kids that he worked with every day, she just had to find the courage to walk through his door.

She was now left standing in the middle of the small living room. It was funny how empty the place felt once he was gone. She walked over to the television and turned it on, waiting for the voices of the morning news anchors to fill the room. She preferred the chatter to the silence, unlike Luke, who wasn't a big fan of the background noise. He had learned to tolerate it to an extent for her though. They had both learned to make a few compromises in the year and a half they had been together, as most couples do. The truth was, there were more differences between them than similarities though. It was a truth they both struggled with when they first started dating, but the attraction was unavoidable. He found her to be refreshing and honest, unlike most of the women he had known. She found him to be safe and kind in a way no man she had ever dated before had been. It only took about a month for them to become inseparable, and Anna found now that she hadn't longed for Collen in a very long time.

She proceeded to get ready for the day and was heading out the door herself about thirty minutes later. She worked only a few blocks away, at the local community college. She lectured three times a week to a room full of mostly uninterested freshman. Many of them were pre-med students, sitting in on the first Biology class of their college career, unaware of the fact that they would quickly change their major at the end of the semester. Regardless of the losses though, Anna loved teaching. For every hundred students that didn't care, there was always one who made it all worthwhile.

She was walking down the stairs when her sister, Alyssa, pulled into the driveway. Alyssa had gotten into the habit of parking her car at Anna's place because she didn't have to worry about paying for a meter. Anna watched Alyssa park, get out, manage to keep her cell phone in between her ear and her shoulder, and then subsequently drop her entire book bag on the pavement.

"Oh crud!" Alyssa cried out. "I'm gonna have to call you back." She violently hung up the phone and looked at Anna.

"Why can't you just swear like a normal person?" Anna said to her, as she bent over to pick up a pencil that was rolling towards her.

Ever since they were kids, Alyssa had hated to swear. She never did it, and Anna never understood it, especially since she could remember their mom saying "shit" and "damn" from the time they were toddlers.

"Anna," Alyssa replied smartly. "Swearing is rude and unnecessary, and I just don't like it."

"Well, tough shit," Anna said as she smiled mischievously at her sister.

"You're not funny! Stop trying to ruin my day!" Alyssa cried out. "It's already a mess! I came out of my apartment this morning and my side view mirror was broken! Someone actually hit it and drove away. They didn't even leave a note! Who doesn't leave a note? That's why notes were invented! I love notes! Don't you love notes? Everyone uses notes! I had to drive the whole way here without being able to see where I was going. It was so stressful." Alyssa's arms were waving frantically around as she recounted her morning to her sister.

"Don't you mean you couldn't see where you'd been?" said Anna.

"What?" Alyssa asked with a confused look on her face.

"It's your rearview mirror. It shows you what's behind you, not what's in front of you." Anna knew she was pushing it, but she couldn't help it. It was just too easy.

"Again. You're not funny," Alyssa replied. She bent over to pick up her book bag, and Anna saw that she was trying not to laugh. Mission accomplished. She had settled her sister down. Anna helped her throw the rest of her things back in the bag and they headed off towards the college. Alyssa was taking classes there while on her journey as a forever student. She had too much energy and love for life to actually settle on a major. So, she just spent every semester finding more classes to take and more reasons not to choose. This had been going on for almost four years now; however, Alyssa's excellent GPA, scholarship, and ability to save money while working as a dog groomer had allowed her such freedom.

Anna's sister wasn't lazy, she could give her that much. In fact, Anna had always seen Alyssa as wise beyond her years. It was funny, being that she was the younger one. In all honesty though, Alyssa had been Anna's rock during her break-up from Collen. She was a reminder of how many other people loved her. Not to mention, Alyssa had a gift for making people laugh, and usually it was just by saying exactly what she thought. Anna had relied heavily on that laughter when she first moved back.

The walk to campus quickly passed, as Alyssa had engrossed Anna in a story about her boyfriend Jess. It always amazed Anna that they had found each other so young. Alyssa and Jess had met in high school. Unlike Alyssa though, Jess had found his passion. Food. When Alyssa started college, he got a job tossing dough in a locally owned pizza place. He had quickly impressed the owners, and a couple of years later, found himself being offered a manager position. The hours were long and the pay not as much as people would think, but he and Alyssa were happy. He was hoping to get enough money someday to open up his own place. First, he had to learn all the aspects of running a store on this own though. Restaurants are notorious for their high turn-over rate. As the manager, Jess found himself training new employees constantly. His latest employee was a nineteen-year-old blond that had quickly become smitten with Jess. Alyssa was not impressed.

"He honestly is so clueless Anna. She follows him around like a puppy dog, but Jess thinks she's just eager to learn. He actually said that too. Eager to learn. Gross! She isn't eager to learn anything more than if my boyfriend wears boxers or briefs!"

"What's her name?" Anna asked, trying not to laugh. Laughing when Alyssa was in a serious mood was not a good idea.

"Who cares?" Alyssa cried. "She's stupid. Her name is *what's-ho-face* as far as I'm concerned."

"What's-ho-face?" Anna repeated. She couldn't help laughing this time. "Please don't tell me you refer to her like that when you talk to Jess. Doesn't that make you sound just a little bit insecure?"

"Of course I call her that!" Alyssa replied back nonchalantly. "How else would Jess know who I'm talking about?"

Anna laughed again, as she and Alyssa walked into the Biology building. "You're nuts. Jess doesn't care about some little girl at the restaurant. He loves you." It was true too. Anna had never seen anyone more dedicated than Jess was to Alyssa. As cliché as it sounded, he thought she hung the moon. What was even better though was that Alyssa felt the same way about him. She never took advantage of his love for her. They were better together, which isn't something most couples could claim to be.

"Well, of course he loves me! I know that! But that doesn't mean I'm blind!" Alyssa replied.

"Alyssa," Anna sighed. "You're going to have to get used to this kind of stuff. Jess is a sweet guy and girls are going to find him attractive." Anna winced as she finished that last sentence, remembering when she told herself the same thing after Collen had started his new job in DC.

"*Where did that come from?*" she thought to herself. It was the shadow of an aching she hadn't felt in a while, but one that had still shown up before nonetheless. However, Anna couldn't even remember the last time memories of her life with Collen had stopped her short in the middle of a conversation. It was unsettling – especially because of how well things were going with Luke. "It doesn't mean anything," she reassured herself. She went through the old ritual of reminding herself that no matter how many aftershocks rocked her unsteady from time to time, Collen was her past. She had survived it and moved on. Although that didn't mean he was erased from her mind completely, it did mean that a random reminder now and again wasn't going to throw her off course. Not now. Not after all this time.

"Anna!" Alyssa cried. "Are you listening to me?"

"What?" Anna asked bewildered. Apparently the conversation she'd been having with herself in her head was keeping her from paying attention to her sister.

"I asked if you thought I should go into the restaurant today to remind *what's-ho-face* that Jess has a girlfriend," Alyssa said matter-of-factly.

"No!" Anna said sternly. "Don't even think about going over there! Jess has a job and needs to focus. He doesn't need you starting a cat fight in the middle of the restaurant with *what's-her-face*."

"You mean *what's-ho-face*," Alyssa emphasized. "And anyway, I thought men liked cat fights," she said mischievously.

"Alyssa…" Anna said warningly.

"Fine, fine, fine," Alyssa muttered.

Anna shook her head. As strong a relationship as Alyssa and Jess had, she was reminded that they were young and inexperienced.

"You have to trust him Alyssa. Without trust, you have nothing," Anna said in a low voice. Lower than she intended, as if she were talking to herself instead of her sister.

"Oh god Anna!" Alyssa laughed. "You sound like a deranged greeting card!" She instantly bounded into a lecture room at the end of the hall.

"See you later!" she called happily over her shoulder.

Anna stopped in her steps for a moment. How her sister could turn off such a serious conversation so quickly was beyond her. To be honest, it made Anna a little jealous. Still in a concerned daze, Anna started walking again and turned the corner to head for her office. It only took a few seconds to reach the familiar door. She took the keys out of her purse to unlock it, and instantly felt at home as soon as she walked inside.

The room was small and crammed with shelves holding an assortment of books, beakers, and plants, but it was her space and she loved it. Alyssa said the room alone was only proof of what a science geek Anna was, but that didn't bother her at all. It was her office. She had worked hard to earn this tiny space in the department and she didn't take it for granted. The only window was small, but brought in just enough light to keep her room bright and the plants growing. It also gave her an excellent view of the pond located in the middle of the quad. Anna looked out and saw that several students had already congregated there. Some were dozing in the morning sun, while others were reading or talking in friendly groups. She smiled to herself and sat down at her cluttered desk, ready to grade the stack of mid-terms she had collected from her students the day before. She had only gotten through a couple of them though, when her mind wandered back to Collen.

She sighed heavily to herself. That was how it always worked. Some random thing would trigger a memory, and before she knew it, his face would fill her every thought. Usually, she shook it off quickly – but today was different. She put down her pen and looked out the window again. Her gaze slowly moved to a tall conifer tree a few feet away from the northern edge of the pond. Of all the places on campus, she loved sitting underneath it the most. She had graded her first stack of papers there. She had eaten dozens of lunches with Alyssa and Luke in its soothing shade. She had even written her very last paper as a graduate student leaning against the trunk – and it was under that very tree that she had officially met Collen for the first time. That day would change her life in more ways than she could have ever known.

In some that she still had yet to experience.

CHAPTER THREE

Anna was twenty-two when she heard Collen's deep distinct voice for the first time. Even after hearing it for so many years, she still had a hard time describing it. It wasn't how his voice sounded, but how it made her feel when he spoke. His teasing confidence always tugged at her heart in a way no one else ever had – and his laugh…when she would hear him laugh, it was strangely seductive, but so easily made her smile.

In truth, it was his laugh that had caught her attention first, because Anna actually wasn't that impressed by Collen when they met. They both attended a weekly ecology seminar where the discussions centered on journal papers and the latest environmental news. As informative as they were, Anna felt as though some people just liked hearing themselves talk. Luckily for Collen, his voice was nice to listen to. However, Anna still found herself often disagreeing with his point of view. It took about two months for her to finally speak up, but once she did, it sparked a conversation that led to one of the best class discussions she thought they'd had all semester. It was later that same afternoon that Collen found Anna sitting under her conifer tree engrossed in a book.

She had sensed him slowing down as he approached, so

she made a point not to lift her face. She didn't want to assume he wanted to talk to her, but she didn't want to encourage it either. She had seen how he interacted with the other women in class. It appeared to her that he appreciated their interest, although he didn't seem to actively pursue conversations with them. Each week, one by one, they had slowly drifted to him...so easily caught up in how it felt to have his attention – even for a brief moment. As intriguing as Collen was though, Anna didn't want to be so easily pulled by him.

After a few seconds, she shifted the position of her back against the tree trunk. That's when he finally spoke.

"Well, hello there Ms. Melone," he said teasingly. "You may not say too much, but when you do, it's definitely worth listening to. I was really impressed by your comments in class today."

As she looked up to answer him, she noticed he had an amused smirk on his face. His brown eyes were intoxicating, but she instantly knew he was trying to bait her. However, as annoyed as she was by his all too obvious attempt to flirt with her through the use of a cheap compliment, she also knew that she didn't want him to leave.

"Let's see what this guy is really about," she thought to herself.

"Oh really?" she said questioningly. "I'm surprised you even absorbed anything I said, seeing as though you seem to be an admirer of your own opinions." She knew the words sounded a little harsh coming out of her mouth, but she couldn't help herself. Anna still remembered his response to one of her comments in class earlier that day and she felt her checks turning red. He hadn't been rude, but his tone hadn't been thoughtful either.

"Is that right?" he said coyly, with an amusement in his voice that now matched his face. He gave her a quick grin and slid his backpack off his shoulder. He moved it down so that it leaned against the side of his leg.

"Yup," she said, trying to act nonchalant and involved in her book. She turned the page quickly even though she hadn't finished reading it yet. As much as she tried to pretend his presence was a nuisance, her stomach was twisted in knots. Anna found herself trying hard not to look into his eyes.

"Well, what did you expect me to do?" he asked. "I'm a man of conviction. I couldn't just let you come in and take my position as head of the class," he said sweetly.

"*You've got be kidding me*," she said to herself. Yet, she knew she was hooked. She wasn't going down without a fight though.

"A man of conviction, huh?" she said halfheartedly. "I didn't realize conviction translated into tossing out condescending comments to fellow classmates when they disagree with your thought process."

That got him. For a moment he looked taken aback, but it didn't last long. He chuckled softly and looked down at his backpack. She could tell he was thinking. It was the first time she had ever seen him at a loss for words. He usually always had the perfect retort. She had seen him in action enough times in class. It had only been a few seconds, but it felt much longer to Anna. As she sat there, she couldn't help but worry he would walk away.

It was then that he finally spoke.

"Sometimes, when a person finally finds their voice, it can be hard for them to not stop talking…and for others not to listen."

He looked up and stared straight into her brown eyes during that last sentence, and before she knew what she was doing, she felt herself start to soften. She couldn't help it. However, she still managed to maintain a confidence on the outside that she didn't actually have. It was quickly withering, but she did everything she could to keep it together.

"Well…," she replied slowly, "I guess that makes sense. I mean, it's pretty obvious that everyone else agreed with me anyway. So I could see why you'd be worried." As she finished that last sentence, Anna closed her book and placed it on her lap. She then looked at him with a wide smile and he burst out with a laugh…that beautiful, intoxicating laugh. As crazy as it sounds, it was at that moment that she started to fall for him.

Anna couldn't help but laugh too at this point. Apparently, based on her response, he took this moment to press forward. "I'm Collen," he said quickly, and leaned over to shake her hand.

"Anna," she responded back with a smile. She gave him her hand for a quick shake, but then pulled it away. She noticed a shadow of disappointment cross his face, but just for a brief second. It seemed to energize him. He lifted his back pack up and gracefully swung it back on his shoulder.

"I know who you are Ms. Melone," he said flirtatiously. She felt something inside her flutter. She stood up and threw her book in her bag.

"So, do you want to go have a cup of coffee?" he asked. "I could tell you about all the other amazing opinions I have," he finished lightheartedly.

She laughed out loud again. She couldn't help it. It was too easy to laugh with him.

"Sure," she said, looking straight into those brown eyes. She sighed quietly to herself, hoping he wouldn't notice the goose bumps on her arms.

"Well then Anna," he said, "I'm all yours."

And from that point on he was – or at least, that was what she was left to believe for the next three years.

After she starting dating Collen, Anna always liked remembering the moment that she knew everything had changed. It was only a handful of seconds, but that was all it took for her to know she had completely fallen in love with him. The only way she could describe it to Alyssa was as though something had shifted. It was as if everything around had stopped and switched direction just for them. It wasn't a momentous moment, in the sense that it wasn't something written of in classic romance novels or played out on a movie screen. It was her moment though…their moment…one she couldn't help but think back on from time to time. One that she always fell back on when she felt as though she needed to remember what real love was like.

They had been spending a quiet evening at Collen's apartment. Since she met him, Anna had to admit that he'd done a good job of making her experience the best that the city had to offer. He had taken her to places she never knew existed – little holes in the wall with nothing but amazing food, music that made her constantly stop and wonder how to find a particular song so that she could download it, and an atmosphere that made her feel both welcome and alive. They would drive out to the mountains and watch the city lights from a distance, talking for hours and laughing at things that were probably only funny to the both of them. He knew so much about everything that she never tired of listening to him. Although, she had to admit that her favorite conversations were when they didn't agree at all, and kept talking over each other to try and get a point across. He was just so damn sexy when he was worked up. Regardless of that though, Anna felt herself filled with an excitement she hadn't known before just by being in Collen's home. It felt good to be so close to all of the things that surrounded him on a daily basis. She felt as though she belonged.

He had just uncorked a bottle of wine. Anna was new to drinking wine. In the past, she had never really liked the taste. It really did seem as though it was something that had to be acquired, as so many have said before her. For some reason though, a glass of wine with Collen was a lot easier to drink than it had been in the past – and tonight…well, it seemed like the perfect touch. As he poured her glass, she watched the red fluid pour effortlessly out of the bottle. He hadn't spilled a drop and none of it trailed down the side. It was a talent Collen said he had obtained while working at his uncle's restaurant throughout graduate school. Anna never really saw it that way though. To her, it was just another thing he could do with a grace and sensuality she had never known.

She watched him swirl the wine in each glass delicately, so that the flavor would come to full fruition. She couldn't help but think of herself, and how all it would take was his touch to make her open up so fully – without hesitation. Anna had to admit that what she had been feeling for Collen the past couple of weeks was completely new to her. It was so overwhelming at times, that it would actually annoy her. It made her feel defenseless, as though she wasn't in control of her own emotions. He had never forced himself on her though, or even attempted to push things forward too quickly. In fact, this was her first time at his apartment. She had to admit that if this was his plan, to keep a slight distance while slowly drawing her near, it was going to work.

"A toast to us," Collen said after he handed Anna her glass. He held his up in the air, and she couldn't help but watch the light bounce off it. The red liquid was dark and inviting, just like his eyes.

"And exactly what are we toasting ourselves for?" Anna asked, with a mischievous look. She always seemed to fall back on juvenile commentary when she got nervous around him. Yet another thing that ticked her off.

"Well, to falling in love of course," Collen said. Before he had even finished his sentence, he had his left arm around her, cupping the small of her back. He was so close. She had to move her arm to the side so that her wine glass wouldn't hit his chest. She looked right at him…feeling everything his eyes were saying and hoping that he felt at least a small portion of what was going through her body. Then again, if he did, she wasn't quite sure if she could handle what would come next.

It was then that he did something she didn't expect. He just looked at her. No words…no kisses…no slow dancing to the music in the background. Nothing. He just looked at her, and Anna could *hear* him. She could actually hear the love in his eyes. It made her heart feel so full that she almost felt guilty – guilty for being so adored by someone. How was it even possible? How could this educated, handsome, fabulous man want her? How had she been enough? It was probably only seconds, but it felt like minutes, and she loved every moment of it. She had to will herself not to look away though. It wasn't because she felt unsettled. It was because she had never felt so fortunate in her life – and in some strange way, that scared her.

The fear didn't matter though, when Collen pulled Anna towards him even tighter. That was when the fear of falling in love turned into the fear of losing him, and she knew that if she didn't soak up every soft touch…every skipped heartbeat…well, then she would regret it for the rest of her life.

That night she finally let go. They stayed up all night making love and talking. When dawn eventually made its appearance, it didn't stop them either. Instead, they skipped all of their classes and stayed in each other's arms. Anna had to admit, looking back on that day even now, that she had never been happier…not before then, or ever since.

That was how she should have known it would never work with Luke.

CHAPTER FOUR

It was taking Anna much longer to grade the tests than she had anticipated. It was already past noon and she was only halfway through the stack. Her distracted mind was not moving the process along any faster either. As she grabbed another paper, Alyssa bounded into her office.

"I'm hungry!" Alyssa cried out in a fake pleading voice. She dropped her book bag, slowly spiraled to the floor, and laid dramatically on the ground. "I think my Psychology class made my brain cells work overtime. The bowl of cereal I had for breakfast is long gone now."

Anna watched as her sister slowly moaned and grabbed her stomach. She rocked back and forth pretending to be in misery. Anna couldn't help but wonder how long it had been since her carpet had been vacuumed, but she decided not to mention that to Alyssa. She didn't want to cut the performance short. Suddenly, Alyssa's hand went up to her forehead and she gave out a loud sigh. Anna knew this was her queue.

"Well," she said hesitantly. "I still have all these papers to grade…" She left the words hanging in the air, acting as though she were thinking hard about what to do. She watched Alyssa's face drop and had to keep from giggling. She knew her sister loved nothing more than a free meal.

"You know, I guess I could break for lunch," Anna finally said, while simultaneously pretending to be distracted by the papers on her desk. "But I really can't be gone too long." As Anna placed her pen in a coffee mug that held way too many old pencils and dried out highlighters, Alyssa bounded off the floor with newfound enthusiasm – her hunger pains no longer holding her down.

"Awesome!" she cried. "Let's go to that burger place down the street. I've been craving fries since yesterday. Some guy in my Economics class brought in a cup of them and refused to share. Rude, huh? I mean, how can you bring something like that to class and not expect to share? It's okay though. Tomorrow, I'm going to bring in some of your homemade cookies and share them with everyone but him!"

"You are?" Anna asked. "And where are you going to get those from?"

"From you," Alyssa said. "You're gonna make them tonight. I'll bring some wine and keep you company."

"Alyssa!" Anna cried out. "What if I'm busy? I can't just drop everything and make cookies just so you can spite some guy. Honestly, why do you even care so much about him anyway?"

"First of all," Alyssa said matter-of-factly, "I don't *care* about him. What I do care about is that this guy is rude, and rude people deserve to get paybacks. Second of all, I want some cookies and this seemed like as good a time as any for you to make them."

"Well, I can give you the recipe and you can make them," Anna replied shortly.

"What?!" Alyssa responded in mock horror. "I can't make them! That's no fun at all! It's only fun to eat them. Geez. You don't know anything." She followed Anna out of her office and watched her lock the door. Anna was trying to think of a reason why she couldn't bake for her sister tonight, but knew she was screwed. Once Alyssa had her mind made up, it was almost impossible to talk her out of anything. How else had their parents allowed her to wander aimlessly through four years of college courses?

"Fine," Anna said. "I'll make your stupid cookies, but you need to bring two bottles of wine. Not just one. Luke is coming over for dinner and he may want a couple of glasses too."

"Yay!" Alyssa cried out. "Cookies and wine! My two favorite things in the whole world!" She danced down the hallway and graciously opened the outside door for Anna. "You're the best sister ever!"

"No," Anna responded. "I'm the best pushover ever. But, who cares? Cookies do sound good!" She smiled at her sister and softly ran into her right side, pushing Alyssa off the concrete path as they walked away from the building. Alyssa quickly recovered her balance and turned around so that she was walking backwards in front of Anna.

"Now come on," Alyssa said. "You still owe me lunch!" She ran towards her sister and grabbed her hand.

Anna laughed and put Alyssa's arm in hers as they walked together, the sun warming their backs.

That night Alyssa kept her word and came over with two bottles of wine. It only took a couple of hours before both sisters were sitting at the table with two wine glasses and a plate of warm cookies in front of them. Anna had only eaten half of her first cookie when Luke walked into the apartment.

"Hey baby!" he said excitedly, as he threw his computer bag down next to the kitchen table and grabbed a cookie. "You will never guess what happened to me at work today!"

Anna was used to Luke's exuberance at the end of the day, but she could tell this was different. She couldn't help and have a little fun with him though. "Hmmmm…." she said teasingly. "They asked you to be the principal!"

"They asked you to be head librarian!" Alyssa yelled out, as she grabbed another cookie, took the last drink of wine from her glass, and then grabbed the bottle to refill it.

"They asked you to direct the school play!" Anna cried.

"They asked you to teach Spanish!" Alyssa responded,

holding her glass of wine in the air.

"No, no, no!" Luke responded. He seemed frustrated, but only in the way someone would be frustrated when they have exciting news to share. "They want me to be part of their teaching abroad staff! They think I have the perfect set of skills to work with international students!"

Suddenly it was silent. Anna could hear the words coming out of his mouth, but she was struggling to comprehend them. Thank goodness her sister, with a cookie stopped in midair, finally found the words to speak.

"Um….but Luke…you're a counselor, not a teacher. And doesn't that mean you won't live here anymore?" she said. The last sentence dropped from her mouth easily, but Anna knew the words meant so much more.

"Well…" Luke responded. He hesitated so long, the silence hurt. His eyes met Anna's and she couldn't help but look away. "They don't just need teachers," he said matter-of-factly. "Kids always need someone to talk to. It doesn't matter where they live."

Alyssa looked towards her sister and Anna knew that even though her heart must have been tugging at her chest, it was time to leave. "I'm going to take some of these cookies to Jess," she said quickly. "And, of course, I need some for class to make rude guy jealous." She started haphazardly looking through Anna's cupboards for a container. Anna couldn't help but love her more in that moment, as she watched her try to make a quick exit.

Luke continued to stand there. He hated fighting and disappointing people. It was obvious to Anna that he was in over his head, but she loved him and didn't want him to be uncomfortable. She knew it was impossible to push away the ever impending words that would fall from Luke's mouth though.

"I have some plastic bags in the drawer next to the refrigerator," she said to Alyssa. Her sister gratefully grabbed the box and pulled out more bags than she needed. Less than a minute later, she had the cookies in hand and was heading out the door.

"I'll see you later sister," Alyssa said to Anna. She grabbed her hand as they walked to the door. When Alyssa turned around, the look she gave Anna was worried but strong.

"Call me later," she said. It was more of a command than a plea, and Anna heard it loud and clear. She watched as her sister walked to her car and climbed in. Once the engine started, she closed the door and looked at Luke.

"How long will you be gone?" she asked. The words hung in the air, but she couldn't take her eyes off him. He looked at the floor, and she knew the answer wasn't good.

"Should I come with you?" she asked helplessly. After what seemed like an eternity, the next sentence came out. "Can I come with you?" The sound of her voice even hurt her own heart. It was so soft. She felt like such a coward.

"Anna," Luke said softly. "You have a life here. I would never expect you to walk away from that. I wouldn't have it."

As the reality of the situation sank in, Anna felt Luke's words slowly sink in too. She had a life here, and he didn't want to be a part of it. Or at least, he didn't need to be.

"When do you leave?" she asked, not really sure if she was ready to hear his response.

"In three months," he answered. His eyes never left the ground. His exuberance was long gone.

She felt the floor fall away beneath her feet, as she struggled to her knees. Her muffled cries were smothered by Luke's shoulder as he held her. Even then though, in that moment, she knew he would still leave – and she hated herself for not being enough to make him stay.

CHAPTER FIVE

When Collen first admitted to Anna that he'd been cheating on her, she didn't believe him. Of course, she had asked him the question, but she honestly never expected his response. Never, in all the time they were together, had she felt anything less than completely loved. He was sensitive, gentle, respectful. How could she even think he would cheat on her?

When she came home after a long weekend visiting Alyssa, she knew instantly that something was wrong. She felt it in every movement he made and in every movement he didn't. He was trying too hard, but at the same time, he was avoiding her. When he finally admitted it, she couldn't breathe. It had to be a joke. She called him a liar.

"No," Anna said firmly. "You would never do that. It's not who you are." She stood helplessly in their bedroom, her hands balled up in fists, her heart pounding in her chest. Still, as the words came out of her mouth, she knew she was trying to convince herself more than him. Because if it was true, what did that mean? What did that make her? An idiot? A fool? She felt the tears coming, but swallowed them back. They were nothing but weakness. She needed to be more than that now. She needed to prove to him that she was worth sticking around for.

It only took a few more moments for her to see the truth though. Maybe it was the way he sighed...it was long, frustrated, tired. Maybe it was the way he looked aimlessly around the room, searching for something to ground him. Or maybe it was the way the light bounced off him, as though he was something cold, that it couldn't touch.

"Why would you do this to me?" she asked him pleadingly, the words tumbling quickly from her mouth, but not as quickly as the tears from her eyes. "I love you. I believe in you. I see you for who you really are." She could hear her voice, but the sentences sounded fuzzy and childish. How could she ever change his mind?

It was then that he changed her life forever. He said something she would never forget. The words were still crystal clear in her memory, even after all this time.

"Anna, I just don't want this anymore," Collen replied. He raised his arms and gestured around the room. "I don't want this life. I don't see myself here."

Anna stood there. Even after those horrible words came from Collen, as far as she was concerned, he was still in front of her – which meant, he was still worth fighting for. So sadly, she didn't walk away at that point. She stayed – and lost herself in the process.

She pretended for three weeks that they could work things out. She made every effort and quickly took away any dignity she had left. She thought it was the way back to him, but Collen hated her for it. He watched every day as she tried to cook the perfect meal. He watched as she bought new outfits and always tried to be interested in every detail of his day. He watched as she lost herself in the imaginary resurrection of their relationship – and finally, he watched as she lost more and more weight from the stress and the worry. He felt her shift constantly in bed every night, unable to sleep because she couldn't let go of the visions of him with other women, not that she would ever admit that to him. Her sadness was so obvious, yet too much for him to handle. They lay there together like that every night. Anna listening to his even breathing, and Collen trying to pretend he couldn't hear the scattered pauses in hers as she cried. They stayed that way until the reality of it all came crashing down one quiet afternoon.

It was a beautiful day…a perfect day…a sunny day…but not for them.

Anna was in the closet, hanging up their clothes, trying to remember what it felt like to feel as though she belonged in this foreign, empty home.

"You know…I'm not going to change my mind," Collen firmly said to her. He was sitting on the bed, the carefully crafted sounds of a guitar coming from the speakers of their stereo…the music haunting and beautiful – just like him.

"I can't make this work."

He looked straight at her, and it took everything for Anna to take her eyes away from the closet and stare back at him.

"I've betrayed you Anna…so many times. Why are you still here?"

The question caught her so off-guard that all Anna could think to say was the obvious.

"I'm here because I love you. I love us. I love who we were, and who we could be…" and then she paused, but only for a moment.

"I know we're more than this Collen," she said sadly – and at that moment, she really believed it.

Collen didn't though.

"No. We're not," he responded coldly. The silence in the room was sharp and felt like knives cutting away at her heart. "How am I supposed to feel about you after all of this?" he asked her. "How could you ever forgive me? As many times as I could hurt you, I think you would always forgive me. What does that say about you? About us?"

It was then that she finally heard him.

A month later, Anna carried the last box out of their apartment and drove back to New Mexico.

Now here she was again, begging a man who was trying to leave her. Did it ever end?

Luke and Anna stayed up most of the night talking about his new opportunity. It turned out that Luke really didn't have to leave so soon, but he had volunteered to. It was a typical thing for him to do – jump to a decision based on what was good for everyone else but him…for them. He was going to a small town in South America, and he wanted to be there with enough time to acclimate to his new home. Anna must have asked him the name of the town at least ten times, but for some reason, she could never remember it. It wasn't because she didn't care. It just made everything too real.

Luke was leaving. How had this happened? She knew his career was important to him, but how could he just pick up and leave her? Didn't she matter? Didn't their life together mean something? The pain of losing him so quickly started feeling too familiar. It was everything she could do to keep it together.

Two days later, Anna met Alyssa for lunch. Her sister could barely sit still as they sat out on the patio of a new local restaurant. Alyssa waited in anxious anticipation to hear the whole story of what had happened after she left. She must have left at least ten messages for Anna since the night Luke made his announcement, but she had only returned her calls that morning. She watched Anna play with her water glass, beads of condensation forming on the sides. Finally, she couldn't keep quiet anymore.

"So…," Alyssa said nervously. "What's going to happen? Are you going to do the long distance thing?" She hated seeing her sister so distracted. It had taken Anna so long to be happy again, and here she was once more…sitting across the table from her, feeling helpless.

At this moment, Alyssa couldn't help but think of Collen. The one man who had made her strong, beautiful sister so weak. It was like a disease. The weakness stayed a part of her. Even long after she moved back home…long after he was gone.

As if Anna could read her sister's mind, she could hear the words swirling in her own. "*He's the reason I don't know how to handle this*," she thought silently. *"How can I even trust my instincts anymore?"* Then Anna finally broke the silence.

"I don't know what to do," she said. A few more seconds passed. "He doesn't think I should go."

Alyssa couldn't help but feel relieved. She didn't want Anna to move away again. She had missed her so much when she left to DC. The anguish on her sister's face was so apparent though. She could feel her stomach turning as she watched Anna continue to stare at her water glass. She was so lost, and she didn't have to be.

"Anna," Alyssa said. "Why are you doing this to yourself? You know I love Luke. He's a great guy, but maybe this is a good thing. Where was your relationship really going anyway? You know he didn't want to get married. You both see things so differently. The only reason you've lasted this long together is because you're both good people who hate the thought of hurting anyone, especially each other. Maybe this is happening for a reason. Maybe it's time to move on." She couldn't believe she had finally said it, but the words tumbled out of her mouth so fast that she couldn't stop them. Alyssa sat there frozen, waiting for her sister to start yelling at her – or worse, to start crying.

It was several seconds later when Anna finally spoke. Alyssa exhaled in relief, having held her breath the entire time.

"You're right," she said quietly, still spinning the water glass in circles as her fingers rested on the side. "We aren't right for each other." It was a truth Anna had known for a long time, but had never said out loud.

She had never been with anyone like Luke before. He had a rare gentleness about him, and was genuinely one of the kindest people she had ever known. He was balanced in a way she had never been – even before Collen came into her life. So, even though she knew there were more differences between them than they knew what to do with, she couldn't bear to leave him. How could anyone leave someone that had never lied, cheated, or made them feel less than who they were?

"I love him Alyssa and I don't want him to leave. I'm not

ready." Anna knew that last sentence was the truest statement of all.

Alyssa nodded her head in silence. Just because it was the right thing, didn't mean it hurt any less. She couldn't think of what to say. A couple more minutes passed. Finally, she said the only thing she knew was true.

"You still have me," Alyssa whispered to Anna, as she reached out across the table and took her hand. For the first time since they got to the restaurant, her sister looked her straight in the eye.

"Yes," she said, leaning forward and smiling at her sweet, little, baby sister. "Yes I do," Anna said. In that moment, Alyssa could have sworn after what had seemed like forever, she saw the real Anna again. Not the Anna of the past two years, but the Anna from before. She was the one that made everything better…her big sister…her hero.

"It's going to be okay," she said confidently to Anna. "I promise."

If she had known what surprises life had in store for Anna next though, Alyssa would have never made such a promise. She would have protected her sister with everything she had.

CHAPTER SIX

Anna and Luke spent the next three months preparing for his departure, but avoiding the obvious. When he left, they knew their relationship would be over, but they never discussed that. It wasn't that it didn't matter. It was that there was nothing to say. For almost two years they had been a permanent fixture in each other's lives, but now…they were moving on. It wasn't in the way that most couples decide to break-up though. There was no chain of events leading up to the end. There was just an opportunity…a chance for Luke to make a difference. It wasn't something Anna could compete with, and it took a couple of weeks for her to come to terms with the truth. She knew it really wasn't about her in the end. Luke was ultimately a good person…a kind person…a selfless person. He was leaving not because he didn't love her, but because his love for her wasn't the point. At the end of the day, his goal was to help kids – and to do that, he needed to go.

Ironically, those last few weeks together, they were closer than they'd ever been. It was as though they were soaking in every moment they could. Anna helped Luke pack up his apartment, and they spent almost every night eating in. They had never eaten out that much anyway, but now it just seemed like a waste to sit in a crowded restaurant and compete with all the noise. It wasn't that they had a lot to say to each other – it was too late for that. They just both preferred the peace and quiet of home. They would sit together on the couch and reminisce about all of the fun times they had, while enjoying a nice bottle of wine and a plate of cheese. Or sometimes, they would just sit together silently – Anna leaning against Luke's chest, listening to his heart beating…wishing two good people could finally catch a break. Maybe they already had though, and now life was trying to give them something new.

Of course, they also spent a few evenings with friends. Luke had surrounded himself with good people, and it was obvious in the way they had all come around to support him during such an important transition. There were a handful of impromptu gatherings, followed by one big party the weekend before he left. It was a fun night, but Anna couldn't help but feel the sadness trying to take over. Later on, after they had gone back to Anna's apartment and were ready for bed, she finally did it. She said what had been in the back of her mind for weeks now.

"Why can't we just try the long-distance thing?" she asked. "It works for a lot of people. Why couldn't it work for us?" To be honest, Anna had several reasons already racked up in her mind about why it couldn't work, but she didn't want to give them any credence. She couldn't help but think that Luke had been brought into her life at the perfect time. It just didn't make sense that this was how it would end. Maybe they were giving up too easily.

Then again, maybe she was hanging on too tightly. At this point, she wasn't really sure what she was supposed to do. It seemed cowardly to just sit by and let their relationship end. That wasn't how it was supposed to work. Relationships ended over something traumatic…something big. Yes, this opportunity was big for Luke, but Anna didn't know how to reconcile in her mind the idea that they went their separate ways over something so innocuous. That, in itself, just seemed wrong.

Luke was quiet for a few moments. Anna knew he was trying to think of the right thing to say. That was one of the things she loved the most about him. He never spoke just to hear his own voice, and he always thought through every word before it left his mouth – so unlike Collen. That was how she knew she could always trust him. He would never mislead her, even if it meant speaking a truth she wasn't ready to hear.

He was so much braver that she was. Anna could see that now more than ever.

They were lying in bed. Anna lay encircled in Luke's long arms. "Anna," Luke said softly as he pulled her in closer to him, his lips against her right ear, "Don't do this to yourself. You don't need to do anything more than be happy. Letting us go is the right thing to do. That's why it's so hard."

She felt the tears slowly start falling. His voice was comforting, but his words were frightening. It was confusing and it only made her start crying even more as she thought about it.

"I just don't understand," she sobbed. "How can it be so easy for you? Won't you miss me?" The tears were really flowing now. Anna sat up quickly and tried to hide her face in her hands, but Luke wouldn't let her. He pulled her arms down and looked straight at her – his blue eyes kind and pleading.

"You are so much stronger than you know," he told her. "Don't let this be something that defines you. What we've had these past couple of years has been wonderful. Of course I'll miss you! But everything happens for a reason. If we let the fear of not being in each other's lives hold us back, in the end, we still won't end up together. You can't cheat life because you think you know better Anna. That's not how it works."

His words were making too much sense, so Anna felt herself becoming angry.

"Don't do that!" she yelled. "Don't counsel me! I'm not one of your students! I'm your girlfriend! You're leaving me behind and it pisses me off!" Now she was screaming. It was too late to back down, so she jumped out of the bed and started pulling on a pair of jeans and a sweatshirt.

"Where are you going?" Luke asked. He seemed genuinely confused, since they were at Anna's apartment after all.

"Why do you care?" she yelled back at him. "You just take off and leave whenever you want. Why can't I?" At this point, she knew she wasn't making much sense. She was letting her emotions get the best of her. She also knew that Luke hated fighting though, so he would let her get away with it. He always let her win. Thinking of that made her even angrier.

She ran out of the bedroom into the tiny living room and starting searching for her car keys. Where the hell were they?! Why did she have to be so damn disorganized? She finally saw them on the kitchen table underneath that morning's newspaper. Luke always took it to work with him and then brought it back home for her to read before bed. She snatched the keys just as he came out of the bedroom. The look on his face said it all. It was an emotion she had never seen reflected before in his eyes. If he could feel that much now, how could he leave in the first place?

Before he could speak she ran to the door and swung it open.

"Anna!" Luke yelled, but the second syllable was cut off as the door slammed behind her.

It didn't reopen.

She climbed into her car and started the engine.

Ten minutes later she was crying hysterically in her sister's driveway. After what could have only been sixty seconds, Alyssa was there. Anna felt her presence even before she felt her sister's hands guide her out of the car. She let Alyssa take her inside where she continued to cry for what felt like an eternity. Not for the relationship she had to let go of though, but for the love she feared she would never find.

CHAPTER SEVEN

When Anna got back to her apartment the next day, Luke was gone. It was a Sunday. He would be flying out in the morning and she couldn't help but hate herself for ruining their last weekend together. She was making everything about her, when it wasn't – not even a little bit. How had she become this person? Luke had never done anything but treat her with love and kindness. Thinking of that now made Anna feel waves of shame at how she acted the night before. She didn't deserve him.

She slowly walked over to the suitcases standing against the living room wall. Luke had packed up the last of his things the week before so that he could stay with her up until he left. Seeing them there brought her some reassurance that he wasn't going to hop on the plane and leave without saying goodbye – even though she wouldn't blame him for doing so. Again, she felt a pang of sadness mixed with embarrassment move inside her.

When the door opened, it only took half a second for Anna to realize Luke was walking in. She ran into his arms before he even had a moment to realize she was there, but he didn't push her away. Instead, he held her. Again, she cried.

"I'm so sorry," she sobbed into his chest. He didn't say

anything. He didn't have to, and yet, she was still comforted.

After a couple of minutes, he guided them over to her couch. They sat down, but Anna couldn't stop crying. Luke handed her a tissue, and at it was then that she couldn't help but laugh.

"Even now Luke…after everything – you're still nice to me," Anna said. Her head was shaking back and forth, as she tried to hide her face in her hands. "I don't understand," she whispered to him.

"Anna," Luke said. "It's simple. I love you."

It took a moment for Anna to catch her breath. It didn't make any sense. She had spent three years trying to be the perfect woman for Collen, but he still left her. Then there was Luke. Even after she acted like a child because he was given an amazing opportunity, he was still compassionate.

"I don't deserve you," she spat out through her uneven breathing. It felt even more true to her after saying it out loud.

"No!" Luke said fiercely. It was a voice that Anna had never heard from him before. "Don't ever say that! Promise me you won't ever say that again Anna. You are more than that. You are more than us."

His words sounded so distant and far away. She had no strength to fight them. She could only agree so that she could try and make him feel better. She at least owed him that much.

"Okay," Anna whispered – her voice still struggling from crying for so long. Even as she heard the word, her heart dropped. She knew she didn't mean it, and Luke knew it too; however, he was up against time.

"Remember. Life knows better," Luke replied. He pulled her closer to him, but couldn't help but feel that she was farther away than ever.

Luke left on a plane at 7:30am the next morning. Anna drove him to the airport and walked him inside, but they both used security as an excuse to keep the misery at bay. She stayed with him as he checked in, and then watched him take the long walk to the security check point. He never turned around – or at least, she didn't think he did. She stood there as long as her heart could bear it, and then turned around and started the trek back to the parking lot. That was when Luke stopped. He put down his carry-on and watched her walk away, wondering if he was fool.

Then again, he knew her heart belonged to someone else. He had felt it almost every day since she had come into his life. It wasn't because Anna hadn't tried. He knew she cared for him deeply; however, he also admitted to himself long ago that she was still fighting to let go of Collen. He couldn't be angry at her for it though. That was how love worked – never on your schedule.

Luke picked up his bag and turned back around. It was time to move on. It was time to be someone new. It was time to let Anna go. As he sat in his seat on the plane though, he didn't feel excitement – only sadness. He was ready for this, but he couldn't help but think that Anna wasn't, and Luke was so afraid that he was leaving her to the wolves.

♪♪

and i can't stay…or hesitate to leave…

you see…

but one more chance to look your way…

— RAY ORTIZ,

"Hesitate"

CHAPTER EIGHT

It takes time to end a relationship, especially after three years and relocating to the other side of the country. Separating bank accounts and updating leases isn't as simple as breaking someone's heart. It requires much more time, scheduled appointments, and the ability to sit side-by-side to sign-off on the disintegration of a life lived together. For Anna though, the hardest part about losing Collen, was waiting to leave town.

It was a couple of weeks before the moving van was set to drive everything she owned back to New Mexico. By then, all of the boxes had been packed up and stacked against the walls. She found herself dreading the last few days in DC before she could finally escape. Even though wrapping up things at work filled most of the hours in her day, Anna had too much time to think, as she was finding it more difficult not to let her emotions get the best of her.

On that day, she decided to stop by the old apartment. By then, she had been staying at a co-worker's house, but needed to grab a suitcase of clothes she had forgotten. As soon as she drove up though, she instantly knew she shouldn't have come.

Calling ahead of time hadn't seemed necessary because she still had a key and it was a Thursday night. Collen always went out to happy hour on Thursday nights, even when they were together. It honestly had never bothered her. At the time, she was proud of them for being in one of those healthy relationships where two people don't have to spend every single moment together. Now, she stupidly realized, that was how he found time to meet other women.

"*It's amazing how the signs are always there, even when you think you were blindsided,*" Anna infuriatingly thought to herself. She sighed out-loud as she nervously sat in her car and looked at the front door.

The problem wasn't that Collen was there. It was obvious he wasn't. The problem was that the apartment was pitch black – too black. He always left a light on in the hall because there was a small table next to the front door that he would run into in the dark. It had only taken ramming his knee five or six times into the edge of the table, to finally pick up the habit of switching on the light when he left in the mornings. Now, the light wasn't on.

Anna's heart sank. She knew right away that Collen hadn't been home in at least a couple of days, and that thought led her so easily to the next – who had he been with?

It really was a meaningless question though, as she had known the answer for a while now.

She got out of the car and fumbled with her keys at the lock. Her hands were shaking so hard, that it took her three tries to finally get the key in the door. As she turned the knob, she had a fleeting hope that somehow she was wrong. That he was there after all. That she could see him, even under these circumstances – because even now, she missed his presence.

When she walked into the apartment though, her fears were quickly confirmed. The signs of his absence were everywhere. The newspaper on the kitchen counter was dated a few days before, and the bananas sitting next to it were so ripe, they had turned an awful shade of dark brown. The bed was made and the pillows were nicely stacked on top. He never made the bed on a daily basis. In fact, he only did it on the weekends. She sadly reminded herself again that it was a Thursday.

As Anna stood lost in the middle of the room she used to share with the man she thought would love her forever, she finally had to be honest with herself. Collen probably hadn't been home in about a week, and he hadn't broken up with her because he didn't want this life. He just didn't want it with her.

She took one last look at the clothes hanging in the closet. There were a lot of empty hangers where some of his favorite shirts used to hang. She felt the tears stinging behind her eyes and her breathing sped up so fast, she didn't even realize the panic attack was coming on. It was then that the misery finally hit her head on. She fell to her knees and cried alone in the dark.

It took Anna about an hour to pull herself together enough so that she could leave. When she finally closed the door behind her, the sound was deafening and echoed across the emptiness in her heart.

It had been four months since Luke left. The first few weeks were the hardest, because Anna kept to herself. She had maintained a sad, lonely routine of waking up, going to work, eating dinner alone, and going to bed. There wasn't much time for anything else in between, because she made sure to draw out those tasks as long as possible. She knew Alyssa was trying to give her some space, but still couldn't bring herself to answer every time she would call. Anna was relishing somewhat in missing Luke, so she didn't want anyone else trying to take her mind off things.

The repetitive silence was broken though every time Luke emailed her. He kept the messages short and simple, but she still waited for them to appear in her inbox. The first email came a few days after he left. He told her about the apartment he was staying in. There were two other teachers from the states living there too, and of course, Luke got along with them instantly. There was no one he didn't get along with though. He made it easy for people to be around him, so he naturally made friends with everyone. Anna couldn't help but imagine what his new friends looked like, how they laughed, what they all talked about as they got to know each other. It made her even lonelier. She couldn't bring herself to respond.

The second email came about two weeks later. It was full of uneventful details about his days there. She could tell he was trying too hard to avoid saying anything that really mattered. She wondered if he missed her, but she was too afraid to ask. She responded that time, but kept the words she really wanted to type locked away.

They went on like that a dozen more times, until the last email arrived. It was only three lines.

"Anna…I know this is hard for you. It's hard for me too…but please, live your life." – Luke

It was as if he was watching her. He knew exactly what she'd been doing all this time and she knew he felt sorry for her. She could almost see sympathy dripping from the words on the computer screen. It embarrassed her that she had used his departure as an excuse to be depressed…to shut down…to fall apart. She didn't want to be this woman. Not again. All of a sudden, her reaction was beginning to feel all too familiar.

She remembered her conversation with Alyssa that day at the restaurant. She had known for a while that things may not work out long-term with Luke. It wasn't so much that they were different though – it was something else. Something she couldn't make sense of in her mind, but that she felt sinking in her stomach. It used to make her feel guilty when he was still around. She had been pushing it away for a long time, but that wasn't an option anymore. It was time to face the reality of what still lay deep inside her heart.

She was never really ready for someone new. She had moved on too fast. She had used Luke.

It made her sick to finally admit it.

Collen had always been between them. From that very first night at the party, he was still lurking in her mind. Yes, something about Luke did inspire Anna that night. How could it not? He was so real…so genuine…but, he was a distraction.

He was put in front of her when she was at her lowest, and although she hesitated, she still turned to him instead of finding strength in herself.

Anna finally realized that she had never really been strong in her whole life. Every memory was a series of mistakes…of missteps…of constant misdirection. It was because of this that she was still alone.

How could love ever come to her, when all she did was reach for anything that hurts?

CHAPTER NINE

It was one of the last afternoons Anna had spent living in the apartment she shared with Collen. Things had been over for at least a week now and several boxes of her things were now piled up in the corner of the living room.

She was standing over the kitchen table, slowly reading the movie section. It was going to be the first time Anna had ever gone to a movie by herself, and she was nervous. What if it was obvious to all of the other couples there that she had been dumped? What if everyone could see how very alone she was? What if she radiated pity?

What if she made it even worse by tripping while walking down those movie theatre stairs that are lit up with tiny, little lights, but that never seem to help the clumsiest person in the world keep from falling over? "*Why do they even have those lights there anyway?*" she thought to herself. They are just a waste of the minuscule amount of electricity they use.

The truth though, was that she was allowing her mind to fill with swirling, meaningless thoughts because Anna was mad. She couldn't help but think of why she even had to go to the movies by herself. "*How did I end up here?*" was the question constantly plaguing her at all moments of the day and night. It consumed her every thought…as if she could change things if she only discovered where or when it was that she had lost him – assuming it was possible to hit the rewind button during the most critical moment of her life.

Most of all though, she was just sad.

All of these thoughts swam through her brain as Anna stared blankly at the newspaper, trying not to cry while repeating encouraging thoughts to herself. *"You are not a loser. You are strong. So what if he wants to sleep around with some stupid whore from work instead of with you? You're better than her."* She couldn't help but believe that she wasn't though.

It hadn't taken much to figure out that he had left her for someone else. In fact, the truth easily revealed itself after one painful drive to the bar she knew he frequented on Thursday nights. After sitting in her car for two hours, feeling every muscle in her stomach tighten to the point where she was afraid she was going to throw up on the floor of the passenger side, she saw him emerge…and of course, he wasn't alone. He was with someone she recognized from his work. He was 100% a walking cliché – and so was she…because she had let it happen.

Anna watched out of the corner of her eye as Collen casually walked over to her right side. She felt her stomach jump. He hadn't been that close to her in days. He had made it a point to keep his distance while she packed. She could smell his aftershave. Its fragrance was intoxicating…like a drug. She felt herself getting pulled to a place that she knew was no longer welcome to her. She placed both of her hands on the table to steady herself.

Suddenly, he was right there…his left arm brushing against her. He knew what he was doing. It was so cruel.

"DAMN HIM!" The words were vibrating inside every cell of her body. Even when he didn't want her anymore, he had to still know she wanted him. It was a sickness. Like the one that was consuming her.

"Hey…are you going to the movies?" he asked.

"Uh-huh," she said, casually enough, as her fingernails dug into the table top.

"Really?" he said. He looked slightly amused.

She closed her eyes and kept her head down, turned towards the newspaper. He wasn't going to make this easy after all, but she couldn't be surprised. He knew her well enough to understand that she never went to the movies by herself, and that she probably hated every second of their conversation.

"What are you going to go see?" Collen asked. He was no longer looking at the newspaper, and she knew he didn't really care about the answer. He just liked watching her squirm. She threw the name of some popular independent movie out as she turned the page. Her eyes locked on a list of apartments for rent. How ironic.

"But I thought we were going to see that together?" he quickly responded. The words just hung there in the air for a few seconds. *Together.*

Anna felt every muscle in her body tighten. Collen quickly moved away to the other side of the table as he messed with his tie. Now he was the one squirming. She could tell he had caught himself off-guard as well. It was a small, but silent victory. It was also short-lived.

"Well that's good," he then finally choked out. "You've really wanted to see that." He finished straightening his tie and grabbed his things as he headed to the door.

Then he surprised her for the second time that day. He turned around and looked at her…his brown eyes locked on hers. She was trapped.

"Have a good day Anna," he said. It was almost a whisper, but the words were wringing in her head. They meant so much more and she knew it.

In a few seconds, Collen was gone. She heard the beeping of his car alarm as he unlocked the doors. She was still frozen at the kitchen table. There would be no movie today. Again, he had defeated her. All she could do was sit and listen, as she replayed the conversation in her mind over and over again.

Anna didn't know how long she'd been staring at the

computer screen. Enough time had passed so that the screensaver was flashing before her – Luke's email now left hiding behind a pattern of ever changing three-dimensional shapes. What she did know was that for the first time in months…years…she felt inspired.

She closed down her email and picked up the phone. It was time to stop feeling sorry for herself.

"Hello?" Alyssa said on the other end of the line.

"It's me," Anna responded. She heard her sister catch her breath. "Can you do something tonight?" she asked. "I want to see you."

CHAPTER TEN

The pity party had finally ended two months before, and since then, things had been very different. After Anna finally reached out to her sister and her friends again, every weekend after that was filled with happy-hour gatherings, BBQs, and outdoor concerts. The weather was perfect for being outside, as summer had departed and the emergence of fall allowed for cooler afternoons and brisk evenings. Anna's favorite time of day actually was the evening. Nothing filled her spirit more than sitting on the patio with a bright, large moon overhead.

She was doing exactly that on this particular evening too. She was over at Alex's house and his fiancé, Cora, had just topped off her half empty glass of chardonnay for the second time.

"Cora!" Anna laughed. "If you keep doing that, you're going to still find me here tomorrow morning! I need to drive home later tonight!"

"What? You finally figured out my evil plan?" Cora responded in a mockingly innocent voice, as she held the wine bottle out to her side. Alex started laughing, as he reached over and put his arm around Cora's waist to pull her closer to him.

"You know love, you really don't need an elaborate plan to make Anna drink," he said sweetly to her before softly kissing her cheek. "She's pretty good about getting tanked all on her own!" he then quickly shouted out, throwing a linen napkin in Anna's direction.

"You shut up!" Anna replied in mock horror. She tried to throw the napkin back in his direction, but clearly missed him by several inches.

Yup – the wine was doing its job.

"It's not my fault that I come from a family who appreciates the fine art of a good drink!" She then picked up her wine glass and toasted the air. Cora quickly held up her glass as well, and toasted Anna's in the moonlight. The sharp sound of clinking glass brought a smile to both of their faces.

"You two are both a couple of drunks!" Alex teased, but he couldn't resist holding his glass up as well – to toast the two women in his life.

A lot of people thought it was strange that Anna and Alex had stayed so close after breaking up. They had only been together less than a year, but it quickly became apparent to them that their relationship was more platonic than romantic. Anna was the first to say that he was one of her best friends though, both then and now. He understood her in a way that only the closest of friends could, and more importantly, he never judged her.

When Alex started dating Cora, Anna was a little worried that she wouldn't be comfortable with their friendship, but she stopped worrying the moment they met. Cora wasn't that kind of woman. She radiated acceptance and ease. It was as though she had always been a part of their inner circle, and she never seemed intimidated by the fact that Anna and Alex had dated. As with everyone else in their group, it made perfect sense that they didn't last. They were friends first, and never really could encapsulate the definition of lovers. It just wasn't the reason they were brought together.

That kind of inevitability Anna would learn of later.

The night sky was intoxicating. Anna could feel a tingling moving through her body as Cora slowly sank into her chair a few feet away. It wasn't the wine either. It was something else…something she couldn't quite put her finger on – but, she figured it was worth holding onto in the meantime.

Why was she always *holding on*?

"So, what's this conference all about?" Alex finally asked. He had settled next to Cora, and his left hand was rested firmly on her back. Anna watched as Cora easily shifted so that she was sitting closer to his side.

Her heart hurt for a moment. Not for the love they shared, but for the fact that she sat across from them alone…

"Well," she said, as she shifted to look directly at them. "It's for work. There are a couple of people from the department presenting their research. It's a really great opportunity to network and support other researchers in the field." She heard the words come out of her mouth, but knew her friends could tell she was holding something back. She hated that kind of atmosphere. Networking wasn't her thing. If she wanted to keep her position as a lecturer though, she had to play by the rules. That's just the way it worked.

"That's cool," Alex replied. His gaze was focused on the sky, but Anna knew he was still listening. "The things we do to earn a paycheck aren't necessarily tied to our ideals. It's not like they define us.

Cora turned her soft gaze over to him and Anna saw a look in her eyes that she knew never mirrored any reaction she ever had towards Alex. It was an admiration she had only ever shown towards Collen.

Cora's hand slid firmly over the back of Alex's neck, and Anna watched as his eyes closed and he drew her other hand to his lips for a soft kiss.

"Damn happy couples," she thought to herself, as she softly coughed at the same time. It was loud enough to bring them both out of their happiness stupor. Suddenly, she had two sets of eyes squarely on her.

"Oh Anna!" Cora replied regretfully. "I'm so sorry! You're still trying to get over Luke, and here we are acting like a couple of assholes!" She quickly pushed her chair further away from Luke and took a long drink of wine.

Luke's reaction was perfect though. He grabbed her chair and swiftly pulled it back in his direction. Anna watched as Cora tried to keep the wine in her glass from spilling over the side. The balancing act she was trying to perform brought a smile to everyone's face.

"*This is not a night for regrets,*" Anna thought to herself.

"No Cora," she said. "I'm done with that...Luke knew what he was doing. All I can do is thank him for having the guts to do what I couldn't. We weren't right for each other." She felt her throat tighten as the words spilled out of her mouth, and Alex must have noticed. He chimed in so quickly, Anna didn't have time to feel the true rush of emotions trying to overcome her. There was still so much guilt...

"Why are we talking about the same old boring crap!" he said sternly as he jumped up from his chair. Apparently, he thought his words would have a bigger impact if he was standing. Anna felt an amused look come over her face, and when she glanced over at Cora, she saw the same reaction mirrored in hers.

"Anna is going to a work conference Cora! Do you know what happens at work conferences! People get over their exes! People hook up! People move on! That's what happens at work conferences!" As he finished speaking, Alex reached for his wine glass and took a quick drink, as though it would officially seal the deal for Anna.

Cora giggled and Anna couldn't help but do the same thing. However, she also felt a familiar pang in her heart. This is exactly why she was still friends with Alex. He knew every emotion she was feeling before she could express it, as well as how much those emotions could overtake her. He was her protector, before anything else.

She looked up at the sky one more time and felt the calm surround her.

"That's right guys," Anna replied with a small smile. "It's time for me to move on." She stood up and walked to the end of the patio. All of a sudden though, she felt cold. A rush of unsettling foreboding swept through her. She tightened her arms around her body so that the warmth of her sweater was pushed firmly against her skin. Cora came up behind her and put her hand on Anna's right shoulder.

"It's okay that it still hurts sometimes," Cora said matter-of-factly. "You don't have to try and hide anything around us. We love you."

Anna leaned her head on her friend's shoulder and felt her muscles release. "I just want to be happy," she whispered. "I think I'm really ready this time…I feel it." Cora reached down and grabbed Anna's hand. Both women leaned against each other in the moonlight, waiting for the inevitable.

Waiting for life to test Anna yet one more time…

The airport was packed. People were everywhere and Anna had to keep moving out of the way to avoid crashing into someone's wayward child, being run over by an off-kilter wheeled suitcase, or having the angriest man in the world roughly bump into her. She could feel the pleasure in his voice as he yelled out that she really needed to find a "new pair of eyes".

It was not the kind of day that lent itself to miracles or coincidences. It was an ordinary day, yet something different was in the air. She chalked it up to the fact that this was the first time she would be traveling alone in a while. There hadn't been many opportunities to do so in the past couple of years. Other than the yearly holiday trips home with Alyssa to see their parents, most of the time, it had been Luke who acted as her companion. He loved traveling and exploring new places. Anna had often found herself being dragged to some new camp site or small town for a quick weekend, where Luke would quickly make friends with everyone and she would pretend to enjoy the outdoors. It wasn't all bad though. On one trip, they hiked out to a beautiful lake and fished all day. It was so peaceful – definitely one of her top ten favorite moments.

The airport on the other hand was far from peaceful today. When she finally made it over to the security line, she realized that the chaos of this day had already taken its course. The line was long and moving so slowly, that people were just pushing their bags across the floor with their feet as they shuffled forward inch by inch.

It looked like it was time for her to pull out her cell phone and find a way to occupy herself. She took it out and found herself skimming through random, saved text messages. At the time, they seemed important, but she had to admit that during the light of the airport day, they appeared a little silly. Most of them were written during an all too real evening of cosmopolitans and rhythmic body-hugging house music, but she didn't care. They came from her friends, and she loved them more than they would ever know. So she kept them, like people keep Christmas cards from someone they will eventually never hear from again, or post-it notes from days long past. She kept them because when somebody cared enough to write them, they weren't worth throwing away.

Anna was still scrolling through her phone when she glanced up to make sure there wasn't too much space between her luggage and the young girl in front of her. It was then that she noticed the dark-haired man in line ahead. His features were so familiar…it was like a reoccurring dream.

The way he held himself…

The way his fingers slid across the cell phone screen…

The way he angled his neck as he read…

She could feel the panic slowly start moving through her. It felt ugly and defeating. The voice in her mind kept saying, "*It's not possible*," but every muscle in her body was telling her otherwise.

She looked over at him again, just to be sure. At least, that's what she told herself…but, it wasn't the truth. She looked over at him again, because she couldn't help herself.

At first, Anna wasn't entirely sure what was happening,

until her body started to ache in a way that she hadn't felt in a very long time. Something that she had been trying to silence for so long had fully awakened, and it was at that moment that the reality of the situation cruelly slammed into her heart.

Collen had found his way to her once more.

CHAPTER ELEVEN

The shot of adrenaline that went through her surprised her so much, that Anna didn't know if she should cry or run.

She hadn't seen Collen in almost three years. He was finishing up a successful architect internship in Washington DC. What the hell was he doing here?

The feelings surging through her felt like a combination of desire and embarrassment. It made her sick to her stomach, and yet she didn't step out of line. She continued to slowly move forward, as she had been doing all this time – and not just today, but every day, since he had left.

It was excruciating.

So the dance continued. Anna watched as Collen moved through the line and turned easily at each corner, glancing up every now and then, but never in her direction. She kept pushing her luggage forward, while he kept moving away step by step. At one point someone in front of him turned around and must have said something funny, because he laughed. The sound of his voice stopped her dead in her tracks. She was frozen. A tingling sensation went through her arms and she knew they had to be covered in goose bumps.

God, that laugh.

"*What am I going to do?*" she whimpered softly to herself

inside her head.

She looked over at him again, but the confusion was quickly taking over any coherent thoughts or ideas.

Collen was now showing his airline ticket and driver's license to the security agent. His back was almost completely to Anna at this point, but she could still see the agent's right arm move up and point him in the direction of the luggage screening line he should go to. She kept watching as he thanked her and put his license back in his wallet. Then he started walking away towards a line that was completely on the other side of the room.

That was when a different sense of panic set in. Not the kind that someone feels when they've finally seen an ex again, but the kind that's felt when they fear they never will.

So, it was then, that she did the unthinkable. Something that she never in a million years imagined doing all the times she played over in her mind how this moment would work itself out.

In the middle of that loud, crowded, security line, Anna called out Collen's name – and not just once, but twice.

"Collen!" she yelled. "Collen!"

She pulled herself up on her tiptoes and started waving her arm, hoping he would see her.

"Collen!" she called for a third time.

At this point, several people were now looking in her direction, including a couple that was standing in front of Collen. Their reaction must have caught his attention, because he turned his head too and finally looked in Anna's direction.

The line had started moving forward again, making it easier for Anna to see him from where she was standing. She waved her arm one more time and it finally happened. Their eyes locked.

Anna watched as recognition took over Collen's face…and then he smiled.

Yes. This was definitely no ordinary day.

Anna and Collen had both managed to traverse the

remaining security checks and were now standing only a couple of feet away from each other in front of what appeared to be a very popular airport restaurant. Anna was grateful that she wasn't seeing him for the first time alone in a silent room, but rather surrounded by the busy noise of travelers and airport announcements. It actually felt normal. Safe.

"Ms. Melone…," Collen said slowly, as though he wasn't sure how to say her name after so long. "I can't believe it's you."

As he said that last sentence, Anna thought for a moment that she heard sadness in his words, but so many emotions were going through her that she couldn't be sure of anything at that point.

"Where have you been?" he then quipped in a teasing voice. He put down the carry-on bag that was slung over this shoulder and opened up his arms – at first hesitantly, and then with the same assurance she had always known to radiate from him.

It was then that Anna finally got her bearings and started to move towards him, her own hesitant smile on her face.

"Hi Collen," she finally responded. She could hear the shakiness in her voice and instantly worried that he could hear it too. If he did though, Collen didn't react. Instead, he pulled her into a big, soft hug.

As Anna stood there in the middle of the airport, smelling his familiar scent again, she felt a wave rush through her. Memories slammed into her mind so quickly that she had to steady herself for a moment, and that was when the inevitable happened. She pulled herself closer into Collen, her arms wrapped around his neck. She felt him rest the side of his cheek on top of her head and felt his jaw move as the words spilled out of his mouth.

"Man, Anna. How I've missed you." His right hand was now resting softly on the back of her head. She felt his fingers tighten a little around her hair.

As Anna breathed him in, she felt as though her lungs had finally filled with air for the first time in years.

"Collen," she said.
It felt so good to say his name out loud again.
"I've missed you too."

CHAPTER TWELVE

They spent the next hour sitting at the restaurant bar talking.

It's amazing how easily someone can put aside so much hurt when they are caught up in a moment they never thought would come – an unexpected moment with the one person that had meant everything. It's usually then that they finally realize what's been moving them forward for so long…the simple, yet incomprehensible, possibility of seeing that someone once more.

At this point, Anna thought a million questions would have been running through her mind, but instead, it was the opposite. She actually didn't know what to say. In a strange way, it was soothing.

To have so much anger towards someone, so much pain…it should be empowering. For Anna though, it was a sedative. She finally had Collen in front of her, and at first, she could barely make it through the small talk.

He asked about her family, and in turn, she asked about his. That conversation topic lasted all of forty-five seconds. Perhaps, that was the intention though.

They then moved on to the ordinary, everyday questions about life in New Mexico and DC. "Weather changed much?"

"Not really."

"Traffic still unbearable?"

"Absolutely!"

"Remember that Thai place we loved? Do you still go there?"

"Sometimes…"

The answer to that last question suddenly stopped Anna's train of thought. "*Who was he going with?*" she couldn't help but ask herself. Finally, a stupid, rambling question to start off the list…and yet, if she was going to be honest with herself, she knew she did have something she wanted to ask him. It was the one question that had plagued her all this time. It had always kept her from ever fully moving on.

"*Why can't I just say it?!*" she shouted in her mind. "*What do I have to lose? It's not like he can hurt me anymore.*"

"*Can he?*"

The words echoed in her mind and it was then that something inside her finally decided to step up.

At this point, Collen turned and looked right at her. For a moment, it seemed as though he was getting ready to say something because he took a deep breath – but then, as he exhaled, Anna saw a feeling of relaxation move through his body. He smiled at her…but it wasn't the same smile she knew from all those years ago. It didn't stop her in her tracks. It actually seemed humbling. It beckoned her forward.

So, she finally threw out the question that had been lingering between them – not only for the past hour, but for the past three years.

"Collen…" Anna asked. "Why did you do it?"

For their one year anniversary, Collen had surprised Anna with a trip to a bed and breakfast in northern New Mexico. At the time, they had been saving for their move to DC, so Anna thought it might be best not to make a big deal of the day or spend a bunch of money. She honestly didn't expect anything special, since they hadn't discussed it – and of course, because Collen was a man. Anna remembered thinking to herself that women are the ones that remind a couple of pending important dates, and that because she hadn't said a thing, nothing would come of this one.

However, she was wrong. Even back then, Collen surprised her.

He turned up at her apartment for what was supposed to be a typical movie night, but instantly let her know this evening would be different.

"Hello my love," he seductively whispered in her ear, as he pulled her in for a long, lingering kiss. Anna couldn't help but think he hadn't kissed her like that in weeks. Her heart instantly skipped a couple of beats.

"Are you ready to go?" he innocently asked, as he pulled her towards him again and devoured her mouth to the point where she could barely breathe.

Anna honestly didn't have enough wits about her to respond, but managed to let out an appreciative murmur as she allowed Collen to move his lips from her face to the left side of her neck.

"I'm ready," she sighed slowly, her arms pulling him closer to her.

"But where's your suitcase?" Collen then threw out mischievously, moving his hands from the small of her back slowly downwards.

He definitely knew how to work her. However, self-awareness finally took over and Anna couldn't help but ask the obvious.

"What suitcase?" she giggled, as she let his hands continue to move to places that were going to quickly make it impossible for them to go anywhere anytime soon.

Of course, it was at this moment that Collen stopped what he was doing and pulled quickly away from Anna. He then planted his hands firmly on her upper arms and playfully shook her.

"You mean you're not packed!" he responded. He then turned her away from him and swatted her on the butt. "Well, you have ten minutes! Get moving!" he shouted, all too happily.

Still unsure of what exactly was going on, Anna stumbled to her bedroom and laughed. For once though, it felt good to be in the dark. She quickly started throwing clothes into a suitcase that she had tossed on top of her bed, but then realized she had no idea where they were going.

"What kind of clothes do I need?" she called out to Collen from the bedroom. "How long will we be gone?" She had pulled a couple of dresses off their hangers and was holding one out in front of her, trying to decide if it was just pretty or if it actually fell into the sexy category.

Suddenly, he was right behind her, with his arms slowly pulling her close to him. "Well," he whispered in her ear, "Clothes really are optional."

The feeling that shot through her body was instantaneous and overpowering. Anna leaned against him and allowed herself to get wrapped up, literally.

About an hour later, she was finally packed up and they were on their way. When they arrived, it was apparent to Anna that Collen had spared no expense. A bottle of champagne was already chilling in the room and two vases of gorgeous red roses were waiting for her – one on the table toward the middle of the room, the other next to the bed. A fire was already roaring in the large, stone fireplace and the voice of one of their favorite musicians was faintly singing in the background. She could hear the notes from his acoustic guitar drifting over her as she walked around the room.

Collen's eye for detail was impeccable. It was what now made him such an impressive architect. Anna knew he must have worked ahead of time with the owners of the bed and breakfast to get everything in place, and she felt her heart fill up with more love than she could ever hold. She still couldn't believe she had someone like him in her life.

She slowly walked over to the vase of roses next to the bed and leaned her head in to smell their sweet scent. When she turned around, Collen was standing there with a look on his face she hadn't seen before. For a moment she got worried, but then he reached out and took her hands.

"Anna, you are the most amazing woman I've ever known," he started. "You are my best friend and I couldn't imagine one day without you. No matter what ever happens between us, I want you to know that." He looked at her so intently, that she almost thought there was something he wasn't saying…but his eyes were bright with a hint of tears, so she instantly tossed that notion aside – preferring instead to believe that it was the honesty of his statement that was making him so emotional.

"I couldn't imagine being without you either Collen," she softly replied. "I love you more than anything. I'll love you forever."

The next three days were nothing less than wonderful. Anna actually found it hard to go back home. She had never felt closer to Collen than she did then, and she didn't want to lose that magic. He must have sensed her hesitation.

"Don't worry baby," he said as he pulled her in for a close hug right before they checked out of the hotel. "We have something wonderful waiting for us in DC. The future lies ahead and I'm so grateful it's with you."

It was one of the first memories she would go back to two years later in order to try to figure out what had been the truth and what had been a lie.

Anna watched Collen look down at the bar top, after the question had finally spilled from her mouth. He was quiet for a few seconds and then he finally answered her.

"In all honesty Anna," he slowly said, "I don't know."

At first, she didn't know what to do with that response. It seemed like a cop-out, but from Collen's demeanor, she could clearly see that he was being truthful. His hand was actually shaking a little as she watched him reach for his drink.

"You don't even know how many times I've asked myself that question over the years," he said sadly. He put his glass back down and then pulled up straight in his chair, as he turned to the right to look at her squarely in the face. He said nothing for a few seconds, until he grabbed her hand and started to stroke the top of it with his thumb. His touch caught her so off-guard that she felt her breath catch in her throat.

"I know I should have an answer for you," he continued. "I know you deserve one, and I'm so sorry to tell you that I don't have it, but just know that it's not because of anything you did. It was never because you weren't enough. You actually were the best thing that ever happened to me."

Their eyes were locked on each other now – her hand still in his. The sounds of the busy restaurant were far in the background, receding with the hurt that she had carried around for the past three years.

It was then that Anna felt a mix of forgiveness and understanding slowly flow into the cracked, broken pieces of her heart.

CHAPTER THIRTEEN

She couldn't stop thinking about him. From the moment Anna sat in her seat on the plane, her every thought was consumed by the conversation she had with Collen. She tried to distract herself with the movements of people sitting nearby, as she watched the repetitive motions of a man across the aisle. He was casually flipping through a magazine, never actually giving himself enough time to read anything on the page, but trying to look busy. Probably because he could feel her gaze on him and was worried she would try to strike up a conversation.

Or maybe it was because he was like her – trying to get his mind off the only thing that really seemed to matter.

She sat quietly for a few more minutes, trying to finally calm the twisting in her stomach after everything that had happened. Then her attention slowly turned to the man and the woman sitting behind her.

"If I could go back in time," she heard the male voice say, "I would have never asked her out. It was stupid for me to think it would work." Anna could hear the frustration in his voice, and could almost picture the sadness on his face. His traveling companion spoke up to offer some words of advice for her obviously conflicted friend.

"You can't do that!" she fervently replied. "You can't

blame yourself. Yeah, it sucks, but at least you tried."

It was quiet for a few seconds, as Anna imagined the man's friend gently stroking his arm or the top of his shoulder – trying to comfort him.

"Would you really not be with her again if you had a chance to do everything over?" she then asked him. "Think of everything you would have missed out on. For a while, you were so happy. Wasn't it worth it?"

Anna found herself holding her breath, waiting for him to respond. It was strange that this stranger's life suddenly meant so much to her, but then again, the thought that someone else was feeling as conflicted as she was right now helped her feel so much less alone.

"Yes," he finally said sadly. "I would do it all over again. I would still be with her if I could." Another couple of moments of silence passed and then he continued. "What can I do? I love her. And if she ever comes back, I'll do everything I can to make it work."

As his words hung in the air, Anna pictured Collen's face in her mind. The conversation between the two strangers behind her continued on, but she had already absorbed what she wanted to hear and was replaying how they had left things.

When they had finally parted ways at the airport, Collen hugged her for so long, that she almost forgot where they were and all that had happened to lead them to that moment.

"Call me," he told her. He reached out for her hand and turned it over so that he could put his business card in her palm. "My cell number changed. The new one is written on the back."

Anna looked down at the card, instantly seeing it no longer as a piece of paper, but as a door back into his life. She didn't know what to do. It was like feeling lost, but found at the same time. Collen must have sensed her uncertainty.

"Anna, I know a lot has happened today. No pressure, okay? I just wanted you to know that I'd love to talk to you again." He reached out and put his hand over hers, covering the business card that sat in-between. "Seeing you today was amazing...I still can't believe it happened."

At this point, they were looking straight at each other. A familiar wave of emotion slowly moved over Anna. It was how she always felt before, when they were first dating. It was a mix of curiosity and excitement that eventually bridged over into love. It was that feeling that helped her finally find her voice again.

"I can't believe it either," she finally replied, "but I do know that everything happens for a reason." She smiled at him and then looked away to put the card in her purse. When she looked back up, he was still watching her. She felt a pang hit her heart as she realized it was time for them to part ways...again.

"Thanks for your number," she said. "It was amazing to see you too." She wanted to say more, but knew it would just be an excuse to prolong walking away. Collen took the initiative instead, by wheeling his suitcase around and looking in the opposite direction. He then started walking backwards, so he could keep his eyes on her.

"I'll be waiting," he said, with a teasing smile on his face. He then turned completely around and started walking in the direction of his gate.

As Anna stood there, and even now as she sat on the plane, she couldn't help but want the do-over her co-passenger mentioned earlier. *"What if this is it?"* she asked herself. *"What if everything really does happen for a reason?"* It was a saying that she had always found herself falling back on when something that made no sense at all happened to either herself or someone she loved. Seeing Collen though had actually seemed to make those words really true for the first time, and that was when she finally knew what she wanted to do.

When her plane landed, the first thing she did was take out her phone and send Collen a text.

"Hi...it's Anna. I can't stop thinking about today. I think I need to talk."

As Anna lay on the bed of her hotel room that night, they talked for three hours on the phone. After the first text, he had responded right away and asked when he could call. She had to admit that it was so nice being on his radar again. When her phone finally rang that night, she did everything she could to sound casual when she answered. She was so nervous though. This was different from what had happened in the airport…*that* was unplanned.

They talked about everything. Well, almost everything. She didn't have the nerve to ask about whatever happened to the woman he had obviously left her for, and if she was going to be honest with herself, she really didn't want to know. Collen didn't offer up that information either. So instead, they talked about work…movies they'd seen…concerts they'd gone to. She found out that he would be traveling to Albuquerque on a consistent basis for at least the next four months because he was consulting on a project there with an old friend from graduate school. When he told her that, her stomach pulled itself into so many knots, she couldn't speak. It didn't go unnoticed.

"Hey," Collen said softly. "Are you okay? I didn't mean to throw too much at you all at once." His voice was so sweet and intoxicating, it grabbed a hold of her even more than she anticipated, but she wasn't surprised. Anna knew what she was getting into when she sent that text. She was pulling Collen back in as much as he was refusing to tug on the line.

"I'm okay," she said sweetly, as her heart pounded in her chest.

It wasn't the truth though.

The truth was that she wanted him so badly, it hurt. It wasn't about sex either. She just wanted to remember what it felt like to lay next to him again – to have his arm across her body. To feel the warmth of his touch…of this presence…of his very need for her too. All of a sudden she felt like she was entering treacherous territory.

"I think I'm just tired," she finally conceded. "It's been a long day…maybe we should get some sleep?" She hated the sound of the words as they came out of her mouth, but knew she didn't have what it took to keep this conversation going. She was too close to saying what she was really thinking, and Anna wasn't ready for the consequences.

"Ok," Collen reluctantly replied. "I understand. Can I call you tomorrow though?" he asked. The inflection in his voice on that last sentence sent sparks throughout Anna's heart. It was at that moment that she believed he really had missed her.

"Yes," she said quietly. "Call me tomorrow. I'll have some time in the evening."

A few moments passed and then Collen's deep voice finally broke out into the room again. "Sweet dreams Anna."

She felt her breath catch in her throat. *How did they get here again so easily?*

"Good night Collen," she finally responded, with a slight touch of desire in her voice. "Thank you so much for calling."

It was his response to this statement that finally made Anna realize where this was all heading.

"You're my best friend Anna," he said. "I've been waiting three years to call you again."

At that moment, Anna tilted the phone away from her mouth so she could cover it with her other hand. She was just so afraid of what she would say. How had things stayed so much the same between them, while the rest of the world had changed? How did she feel so many emotions for him, even now?

As those questions echoed through her mind, she prepared herself not to give too much away.

"Good night Collen," she finally replied for the second time – but even then, she couldn't just leave it at that. She had to say more.

"I'll be thinking of you."

The words lingered between them over the phone connection, until Anna hung up. She knew without a doubt that no matter how much strength she had, she was right back where they had started that first day at the conifer tree. She could feel her love for him coming back to the surface…a love that had never really left her. A love that was a door to what she thought was a second chance.

CHAPTER FOURTEEN

The week of the conference went by in a blur. The reality of the situation though, was that Anna's attention was not focused on research seminars, but instead was completely wrapped up in Collen. He had been calling her every night, each conversation lasting as long as the first. She loved every minute of it too, regardless of the lack of sleep. If she wasn't on the phone with him, she couldn't sleep anyway. Her mind was swirling with too many thoughts and emotions for her to turn it off.

When she flew back into town, she felt like a new person. The very fact that Collen was back in her life gave her a confidence that she hadn't had since driving away from DC. Even though they hadn't talked at all about what it meant to actually be talking, all that mattered to her was that they were.

There was something that she was very nervous about though. It had been lingering in the back of her mind since she first ran into Collen again.

How was she going to tell her sister?

Alyssa had been the one to drop her off at the airport, and she would be picking her up at any minute. As Anna stood on the sidewalk outside the arrivals section, she felt her heart pounding in her chest.

She could never lie to Alyssa. She was a horrible liar in general, but when it came to her sister, all bets were off. Alyssa always knew when she was hiding something, and Anna had no doubt that as soon as she stepped into the car, Alyssa would be able to see that something had changed. When she found out the truth, Anna also knew that she wouldn't like it. In fact, nothing could make Alyssa angrier than talking about Collen. She hated him. As hurt as Anna had been when she moved back, she was actually grateful that he lived on the other side of the country so that her sister wouldn't have the opportunity to let him know exactly how she felt. It wasn't that she had been trying to protect him from hearing the truth of Alyssa's words. It was just that too much ugliness had already surrounded the entire situation. All she wanted at the time was for it all to stop.

Anna finally saw her sister's car down the road. She really wasn't ready to share this news with her. She wanted to keep it safe to herself, where others couldn't judge her – or judge Collen, for that matter. She knew that people wouldn't understand why she had allowed him back in, but at least her friends would listen to her reasons. They would try to be supportive. Her sister on the other hand would not be so patient, and Anna never handled confrontation with her well.

What she really wanted to do was wait and see where all of this was leading first, because to be honest, Anna wasn't even sure what to say to Alyssa. That she had run into Collen? That they were friends again? That he was working here?

That she had forgiven him?

The last part would make Alyssa the angriest of all.

As it turned out, Anna was worried for nothing. When her sister picked her up, she could tell they wouldn't be talking about her trip or the encounter she had at the airport days earlier. She could tell that something was horribly wrong.

Alyssa's face was red and blotchy from crying. She didn't even look directly at Anna when she got in the car, but she could see the tear streaks on her right cheek.

"Oh my God!" Anna cried out. "Alyssa! What's wrong? What happened? Please talk to me! Are you okay?" She felt the panic move throughout her body as a million thoughts swirled in her mind. Was it their parents? Did something happen to one of their friends? Was someone sick? She wanted to reach over and hug her, but Alyssa looked so small and fragile. The pain was so obviously embedded in her face and her arms were stiffly attached to her hands, which were forcefully clamped onto the steering wheel.

"What's going on?" Anna pleaded. "You need to say something to me! I'm freaking out right now!"

Alyssa still wouldn't look at her, but it was then that she finally spoke.

"Just give me a minute, okay?" she quietly replied. "I just need a minute." Then she let out a sigh that sounded more like a whimper because her breathing was still shaky from whatever awful truth had made her cry.

Anna waited as her sister drove them away from the airport and got onto the highway. She didn't know how Alyssa could even see, as her eyes were obviously still blinded by tears. Anna stayed as silent as she could, even though she could feel the tears building in her eyes too. She couldn't help it. Her sister's grief was too much for her to take, and she didn't even know what had happened yet.

Alyssa finally pulled over. They were only a couple of miles from Anna's apartment, but it was obvious that she was done driving. As she pulled the car to a stop, Anna felt her heart sink.

The silence was unbearable, but she didn't say a thing.

Then finally…the truth.

"I kicked him out," Alyssa said. It was only four words, but the weight of their meaning hung in the air like a thick fog.

"What?" Anna whispered. She knew she had to sound like a child, but she was clearly at a loss for words. Could she have even heard her right? "You left Jess?" Anna finally said, the confusion apparent in her voice. The words almost got stuck in her throat, but she wasn't going to let them stay there. She had to be the strong one for once.

"Yes," Alyssa said firmly, her hands still grasping the

steering wheel of the car. "I had to," she finally elaborated.

Another moment of silence followed, making it impossible for Anna to stay patient any longer.

"Why?" she asked hesitantly, as she put her hand on her sister's arm. "Alyssa, I don't understand what's going on."

Alyssa looked out the car window at that point, but still didn't say more. The sadness in the air was drowning them both. Anna felt another wave of tears coming, but held them back. This wasn't her moment to cry.

"He cheated on me," Alyssa said matter-of-factly. "I caught him."

Anna gasped and looked uncomfortably around the car, as if an answer to why this was all happening would materialize. She then felt the weight of the situation settling in, as she finally stared at her sister.

Horribly enough, she knew exactly how she felt.

"How did you catch him?" she cautiously asked. It was an awful question, but there was no way around it.

Alyssa sighed, but Anna knew she would tell her everything.

"I went to the restaurant to surprise him at lunch," she slowly started. "He's been kind of grumpy lately, but he's also been working a lot. I've actually hardly even seen him the past couple of weeks. So, I thought it would be nice to stop by and see if he wanted me to pick him up something to eat. I know he gets sick of having pizza all the time." At this point, Alyssa stopped talking, released the steering wheel, and put her hands in her lap. Anna saw they were trembling. Her sister, always trying to remain in control, quickly hid them under her thighs and went on.

"I didn't even think about knocking on the office door. I just walked right in...and that's when I saw them."

Anna reached out to touch her sister again, but then pulled back. She hated every moment of this, as she knew it was killing Alyssa; however, she could also tell that she wasn't ready to be consoled yet. It was only a couple more seconds of silence, and then Alyssa went on.

"They were kissing," she softly whimpered. It was obvious she was replaying the memory in her head, because she stopped sitting on her hands and put them over her eyes.

"Was it *what's-her-face*?" Anna couldn't help but ask. It was then that she had to ask herself, what if Alyssa had been right not to trust that girl all those months ago.

"No," Alyssa said sadly. "It wasn't her. It was someone else. I've never seen her before. She doesn't even work there."

"What?" Anna responded, even more confused than she was before. "What do you mean she doesn't work there? Where the hell did her meet her then?" Now she was getting angry, but it was nowhere near how angry Alyssa was about to get.

"Anna! I don't know where he met her!" Alyssa yelled out. "I don't give a crap! All that matters is that Jess is a scumbag and he's been cheating on me with her for a month now!" After those last words rushed out of her mouth, Anna watched as the tears started flowing again. She leaned over and finally pulled her sister in for a hug. Alyssa was crying so hard now, that Anna could feel her entire body shaking against hers. Neither one of them spoke for a few minutes, until Alyssa finally pulled away to grab a tissue from her purse.

"So…" Anna finally said hesitantly. "What does Jess say about all of this? Did he explain himself?"

"What is there to explain?" Alyssa said smartly. "He cheated on me. We're done. That's a deal-breaker." The tissue she was holding in her hands was already soaked through, so Anna pulled out her purse and grabbed a few more from a new package she had picked up before going out of town. As she held them out for her sister to take, she couldn't help but ask one more question.

"Well, did he actually sleep with her?" As soon as the words came out of her mouth though, she wished she could take them back. Her sister was glaring at her with wide eyes…the anger etched in every part of her face.

"And what is that supposed to mean?" Alyssa shot back. "That if he didn't sleep with her it's okay? Are you seriously that stupid? He's been screwing around on me for weeks now Anna! He admitted it! And yes, since you must know, he has been sleeping with her! That's why he's been acting like such a jackass! He said it's because he's been feeling guilty, but that sure didn't stop him from continuing to do it!" With that, Anna watched her sister start the car up again.

"Alyssa," Anna quickly said. "You should let me drive. You're too upset. Please. I don't mind." Her sister's response made her quickly realize she had said the wrong thing again though.

"NO!" Alyssa screamed. "I can freaking drive Anna! Just shut up!"

Anna felt like the wind had been knocked out of her, but she knew her sister had a million emotions rushing through her at the moment. She needed to just let her feel them.

They drove the last couple of miles together in silence. Anna could feel the fury radiating from Alyssa, so she didn't ask the other dozen questions that were scrolling through her mind. Her sister was obviously done talking about what happened.

When Alyssa pulled up in front of the apartment, Anna didn't know what to do. Should she get out and leave things like this? Did Alyssa even want her help anymore? Should she take a chance and ask her to come inside? Everything about the situation was so overwhelming, and nothing had even happened to her! It had happened to her sister!

She felt so helpless.

Then Alyssa spoke.

"I'm so sorry Anna," she said sadly. "I shouldn't have been so mean. I know this doesn't have anything to do with you. I just never thought I'd be here." That last sentence Anna understood all too well.

"You don't think there's any way to fix things?" Anna quietly asked. It was an obvious question, so she hoped Alyssa wouldn't find it infuriating.

"He wants to work things out," she slowly replied. "He said it was all a horrible mistake and that he'll never do it again."

"Did he explain why he even did it in the first place then?" Anna asked.

"Well," Alyssa replied, "That's the stupidest part of all. He says he doesn't know why he did it. Can you believe that?" She then threw her hands up in the air in obvious frustration.

Unfortunately, Anna could believe it as she immediately thought back to her conversation with Collen in the airport. So, of course, she had to try and come up with a good reason for that kind of response.

"Maybe he's telling the truth," she finally said. "Maybe he realizes now how ridiculous he was acting and he just wants to make things right. You could still have a chance to work things out. It could be worse."

The silence in the car after that last sentence was deafening.

"You mean, at least this break-up doesn't mean I have to move out of town?" Alyssa responded coldly.

"*Damn it*," Anna quietly thought to herself. "*You're on a roll today.*"

"You know Anna, everything isn't always about you," Alyssa said on the brink of tears again. "Yes, come crappy stuff happened to you in DC, but that doesn't make you the queen of bad break-ups! It doesn't make my situation any less awful!"

Anna was stuck. She knew Alyssa had a point, but she honestly didn't know how to respond to such heated words. So instead, she didn't say anything.

"You need to get out of my car now!" Alyssa angrily yelled.

So Anna did.

She watched as her sister drove away in a rage, but instead of feeling worried, she actually felt relieved to not have someone yelling at her anymore. She turned to her apartment and slowly started going up the stairs. All of a sudden, she felt exhausted. After opening the front door, she threw her suitcase in the middle of the living room floor and reached inside her purse to pull out her cell phone.

Collen had texted her three times. He wanted to make sure she had made it back safe.

The wave of happiness that Anna had flown back into town on quickly washed over her again. She felt the urge to call him right away, but was disappointed when he didn't answer. She really wanted to hear his soothing voice after everything that had just happened, but she figured he was probably working. She put her phone down on the kitchen table, sat down, and stared at it.

She was contemplating calling Alyssa, but she knew her sister all too well. She needed time to cool off. It was probably better to wait a few hours.

Suddenly, her phone rang. Anna's heart jumped when she saw the number. It was Collen. She quickly answered.

"Hello?" she sweetly said.

"Hey baby," Collen responded just as warmly. "I finally get to hear your voice."

Just like that, Alyssa was far from her mind.

CHAPTER FIFTEEN

Even though she called and text messaged every day, Anna didn't talk to her sister for a week. She had to admit that she wasn't surprised Alyssa had been avoiding her. It had always been obvious to her that they handled stressful situations very differently. Although Anna found it easy to lean on others and talk things through, Alyssa was the complete opposite. She would hide and try to deal with things on her own. Anna realized now that it was amazing she had even told her about Jess in the first place. If she hadn't already promised to pick her up from the airport, Anna probably wouldn't have known for days that they had broken up.

Alyssa's ability to avoid people when she's upset, compounded by the fact that Anna had done a tremendous job of pissing her off, made it very easy to understand why it took her a few days to finally respond. Anna believed that deep down, Alyssa had lashed out at her only because she was frustrated and had no one else to take it out on, but she was also confused. Everything had happened so quickly. It was as though there was something more…something she had missed.

Normally, Anna would have been sick over the fact that they weren't talking. The reality though, was that she was too preoccupied with Collen to agonize about it. A couple of days after she returned from the conference, he told her he would be flying back for work sooner than expected. He was hoping to come in on a Friday too, so that he could spend the weekend with her.

"So, what do you think?" he asked her during one of their marathon phone calls. "Are you ready to spend some time together in person for once?" His voice had a teasing hint to it, but she could tell he wasn't entirely sure what she would say.

The answer was easy though.

"Of course!" Anna responded joyfully. "Was there anything in particular you wanted to do?" She was already thinking of a couple restaurants he would like that had opened up in the past year, and there was also a new exhibit at the natural history museum.

"Well," Collen started slowly. "I thought maybe we could check out that bed and breakfast again. Do you remember it? The one we went to before we moved?"

Anna's stomach lurched at the thought of being there with him again. A flood of memories from that weekend flew through her mind, but unlike how she'd been feeling the past couple of weeks, this time she was left with a hollow, empty feeling. Other than their first conversation at the airport, she had tried to avoid talking about the past. It had been easy enough to do, since they were both enjoying the rush of being back in each other's lives. Who would want to ruin that by rehashing their break-up?

The obvious truth though, was that the thought of going back to a place that once before had meant something special to them scared Anna. It seemed too easy to start down an all too familiar road that ended in an all too familiar way. If this was going to be a true second chance, she knew they needed to start fresh in every way possible.

"Collen," she softly said. "It means a lot to me that you remember how much we loved that trip, but I honestly think we need to be careful about trying to recreate the past. We've already come this far. We should keep moving forward. Don't you think?" Her heart was pounding now. The fact that Collen had even wanted to go away with her finally starting sinking in and Anna started to feel light-headed. Everything was happening so fast, and they still hadn't even discussed what any of this really meant.

"*What am I doing?*" she thought to herself. As soon as Collen spoke though, the words fell out of Anna's head, leaving behind the faintest shadow of a doubt. The kind of doubt that is so easily pushed aside, that even when you think back on it later, you can't be sure it was ever there.

"I agree with you a hundred percent," he kindly responded. "And you know what?" he added, "We don't need to rush anything. Let's wait to talk about going out of town. For now, I'm just looking forward to sitting across from you and looking into those big, brown eyes."

Anna felt her fingers tighten around the phone as she held it to her ear. Collen had slightly lowered his voice during that last sentence and its seductive tone had clearly impacted her. It was going to be really hard to wait the next few days until he arrived in town.

Alyssa's reemergence was probably the only thing that could finally distract her from the upcoming visit. So, when her sister's number finally lit up Anna's cell phone screen, she eagerly answered it. Even if she was about to be yelled at, it would be worth it to hear her voice.

"I'm really sorry you haven't heard from me," Alyssa instantly said when Anna answered the phone. "I was a mess the other day, but I didn't realize how upset I really was until I completely turned on you. It's just been so hard Anna. Harder than I thought it would be…you know?" It was as though Anna could actually see those last two words hovering in the air – directionless, lost, just like her sister.

"I understand," Anna said softly. "Why don't you come over? Let's talk."

Less than thirty minutes later, Alyssa was knocking on Anna's door. The moment she swung it open, her sister ran into her arms.

"He's gone!" she cried into Anna's shoulder. "He picked up the last of his things yesterday and he's not coming back. He's not coming back Anna…" as the words fell from Alyssa's sobbing mouth, Anna instantly felt the weight of them – as though they belonged to her. Perhaps they did, since she had reconciled long ago that her and Alyssa were one and the same. No matter how they handled life's dramas.

"It's going to be okay," Anna whispered into Alyssa's ear. "I promise. Life knows better."

Suddenly, she felt her sister completely let go, as she sank into her arms and let out one last wail. There was no way to know how long she held her, as time didn't matter at this point. All that mattered was that Alyssa needed to find herself again. She needed to know that she was more than this – as anyone would when their heart had been broken.

After some time had passed, Alyssa finally sat up and looked at Anna. What she said next surprised her more than she ever anticipated. She knew her so well.

"You're different," Alyssa simply stated as she wiped the last remaining tears from her eyes. Tears that Anna knew would have few future acquaintances – tears that were actually shed as a final memorial. "Something's off. What's going on?"

That last sentence struck Anna so hard, she would have sworn it wasn't made up of only words. She instantly wondered how Alyssa had picked up on something. Even in the middle of this hell, she knew things weren't quite right.

Anna had no idea what to say, so instead, she fell back on the first thing that came to her mind.

"I'm fine," she responded to her sister. "I've just been so worried about you. I honestly never thought this would ever happen."

Okay. Maybe it wasn't a total lie, but the absolute truth definitely was not in the cards at this point. She could only hope Alyssa wouldn't press the issue.

"It's been so hard not to talk to you the past few days," Anna continued. "You were completely ignoring me! That's never happened before!" At this point, she reached out and took her sister's hands in hers. "I just want you to know that I'm always here for you."

Alyssa looked at her hesitantly for a moment, and in those few seconds, Anna tried to prepare herself. She knew she couldn't keep what was going on with Collen a secret. She needed to come clean. She watched Alyssa's eyes leave hers and slowly look around the room. She could tell she wanted to say something, but no words came out. Instead, she pulled her hands away from Anna's and stood up.

"I've decided to go home Anna," she finally said. "I need some time to think and I can't do it here. I'm leaving in a couple of days."

Anna knew she should offer to come, but Collen was coming into town that weekend. So instead, she quickly convinced herself that her sister would be in good hands with their parents.

"Well," she replied. "I think that's a good idea. It might help you figure out the next step."

Then again, her sister surprised her.

"Oh no," she quickly said. "I know what the next step is. I just need to make sure mom and dad are okay with it."

"What?" Anna responded in a frustrated voice. "You know what you want to do? Why won't you just tell me then? This is ridiculous!"

"*This* is ridiculous?" Alyssa forcefully spat back. "You are obviously hiding something from me, but I'm the bad guy?"

Anna was stunned. It was apparent that time had run out, but yet, she still couldn't find the strength to tell her sister the truth. So she took the coward's way out and did something she never could before – she flat out lied.

"I have no idea what you're talking about!" she yelled back cruelly. "You're obviously completely paranoid from what's been going on! You need to leave me out of this!"

"Oh, really?!" Alyssa screamed back. "I'm paranoid? Or maybe I'm just mistrustful? I'm making this all up in my head, right? Nothing's going on with you?"

Anna was at a loss and had no idea how to respond. She

felt a lump start forming in her throat and she knew with absolute certainty that she had definitely missed something after all. Her hands were balled up in fists at her sides as she stared at her sister, trying to figure out her next move.

"Well?" Alyssa said in a frustrated voice. "Aren't you going to say anything?" Anna watched as Alyssa's eyes welled up with tears again, and the guilt slammed into her heart like a wrecking ball. The time it was taking to search her mind for the perfect words though was misinterpreted by Alyssa as prideful silence, and her sister finally lowered the boom. Anna watched her walk over to her purse, pull out her phone, and start searching through it.

"What are you doing?" she asked Alyssa in a confused voice. She started walking towards her sister so that she could get a look at the screen, but it wouldn't be necessary. Alyssa found what she was looking for and held the phone up to give Anna a clear view.

"Who's mistrustful now?" she spat out.

Anna reached for the phone so she could get a closer look at the string of text messages displayed on the screen. She quickly scanned them, but as she tried to make sense of what was going on, one text finally jumped out at her. It was a text that was never meant for her sister, and it was very clear to her now what was going on.

How could she be so stupid?

"Go ahead," Alyssa prodded. "Read it."

As the reality of the situation hit Anna, all she could do was feel sorry. Sorry for herself because she had lied to her sister in the first place…but also sorry that Alyssa had to finally confront her.

"Alyssa…" Anna sighed. "I know I should have told you. I just didn't know how." She looked straight into her sister's face and watched it turn red with anger.

"Oh!" Alyssa said in an annoyed voice. "But you did tell me Anna. You just didn't realize you had." The words were dripping with sarcasm. "Now what exactly did you say again?" She then grabbed the phone out of Anna's hand and started reading out loud.

"Aren't you cute? I wish you could pick me up too handsome. As soon as Alyssa drops me off though, I'll call you."

It was from a run of text messages Anna and Collen had been sending back and forth to each other the night before she flew back from the conference. There had been so many though, both before it and after, that it wasn't missed. Unfortunately for her sister, during that conversation, she had also text messaged Anna. She needed to double-check with her about what time her flight was getting in, so that she knew when to pick her up. Anna had responded to that text correctly, but obviously didn't do a good job of keeping the two conversations straight and replied again to Alyssa when she was really talking to Collen.

Yes. She really was that stupid.

"How long have you been talking to him?" Alyssa asked in an irritated voice.

Anna was finally done with the lies.

"It's been a couple of weeks," she responded sadly. "How did you know it was him though?" She knew the answer, but she still couldn't help but ask the question – in a strange way, it was a comfort to her in the middle of this awful dialogue to be reminded of how well her sister knew her.

"Who else would it be?" Alyssa smartly replied. "You haven't talked to Luke in months and I know you weren't seeing anybody before you left. You also didn't call me once while you were gone – probably because you were too busy sending love-struck messages to that jerkoff. He's the only person I know who has ever high-jacked you from the rest of the world. Speaking of that…exactly how long did it take you to call him after I dropped you off the other day? Thirty seconds? A minute? It was pretty obvious to me that you didn't seem to mind getting out of the car, even though I was a crying, screaming mess."

Anna knew there was no way she was going near that question, but she did have something to say.

"So, this is why you were so mad at me the other day? You've known all this time that I'm talking to Collen again. Why didn't you just say something?" Anna was now sitting solemnly on the living room couch. As she stared at the ground, she wished she could be anywhere else.

"Because I shouldn't have to!" Alyssa cried out. Her voice was getting loud again and Anna could tell the yelling wasn't over. "I thought we talked about everything!"

"When was I supposed to tell you?" Anna replied. "You were so upset the other day. I was supposed to bring it up then?"

"No!" Alyssa yelled. "You should have told me when you guys first started talking! You shouldn't have sat on it, like some kind of dirty little secret! But you did! And when I told you what was going on with Jess, as much as I know you wanted to help that day, all I could think of was that even after Collen did the same damn thing, you let him back in. It made me crazy! Do you even have any idea what you're doing?"

Of course, Anna had no idea what she and Collen were doing, but she wasn't going to admit that to Alyssa.

"We haven't really talked about that…" she started. "We're just getting to know each other again."

"What the hell is there to know?" Alyssa replied crossly. "He's a jerk Anna! How do you not see it?"

Even though she knew it was only going to make things worse, Anna couldn't help but defend Collen.

"People change Alyssa," she said. "I've forgiven him. That was the past. I don't want to go back there anymore. I want to see where things can go, if we have a fresh start."

"But we're supposed to learn from the past," Alyssa responded. "Not ignore it. You're smarter than this Anna. He doesn't deserve a second chance with you!"

"Don't do that!" Anna shot back. "I don't want to fight with you about this Alyssa! Why can't you just let me do what I have to do?"

"Because what you're doing is ridiculous!" Alyssa yelled. "And it's wrong! It's already turned you into a liar!"

"I'm not a liar!" Anna screamed. "So, I didn't want to tell you! Can you blame me? Look at how you're reacting! This isn't your life! It's my life and I know what I'm doing!"

"Oh really?!" Alyssa shouted. "Well you know what? Whenever anybody has to say that they know what they're doing, that is just proof that they have no idea what they're doing!

"Are you done?" Anna harshly replied. It was now very evident that Alyssa was not going to listen to anything she had to say, and she no longer wanted to hear her bad-mouth Collen. She loved that he was back in her life, and she wasn't going to feel guilty about it.

"Yes," Alyssa said – her voice as cold as steel. "I'm done. Sorry to have bothered you." With that, she turned around and walked straight to the front door.

"Alyssa," Anna said sadly. "Wait."

Alyssa took her hand away from the door handle and turned her head to look at Anna.

"Have a safe trip, okay?" Anna quietly said. She watched as a look of pure exasperation washed over Alyssa's face.

"Whatever," she replied as she opened the door and slammed it behind her.

As Anna stood there, she could hear the words they had shouted at each other still echoing in the now silent apartment. It was then when she realized that even with Collen back in her life, there was still room for a different kind of heartbreak.

♪♪♪

all i thought that we'd be makes me fall again to you…

                     – RAY ORTIZ,
                        "Fall"

CHAPTER SIXTEEN

Anna had to admit that she felt like a weight had been lifted once she knew Alyssa was out of town. Collen would be arriving soon and she couldn't help but feel grateful that she didn't have to worry about her sister confronting her again while he was there, but she did need to talk about what had happened. So, she called her friends and invited them over for dinner the night before Collen was supposed to fly into town.

Matt, Lila, Alex, and Cora had all spent time together before, and with Alyssa gone, they were Anna's foundation. So, she knew if she was going to finally open up to anyone about how she was feeling again for Collen, then it would have to be with the four of them.

As she cleaned her apartment and started prepping for dinner, her mind raced to find the perfect words. She still didn't know how she was going to tell her best friends that Collen was back in her life. They had been nothing but supportive and understanding when she came home. They never once made her feel stupid for the decisions she had made before…but what if they couldn't back her up on this one? Alyssa couldn't. Would they feel the same way?

It wouldn't necessarily be a choice between them and Collen, but she was so worried that after all of the late night conversations and the "you'll get through this" pep talks, they would respond negatively to the simple fact that she was seriously considering a romantic relationship with him again. Would it seem like a slap in the face?

Actually, if she was going to be completely honest, they definitely were already involved again. Regardless of the fact that they had not been physical and she had only seen him that one time in the airport, her emotions and her heart were with him all the time.

A couple of hours later, Alex and Cora arrived. They were always on time, which Anna loved because out of all of her friends, their consistency never faltered. She knew she could always depend on them, as they so easily could with each other.

"We brought wine!" Cora happily called out as she held the bottle up and walked through the front door into Anna's small, but cozy, living room.

"And…we brought a back-up!" Alex replied with an intermingled laugh as he held up a second bottle and followed closely behind Cora. They both quickly crossed into the kitchen and placed both bottles next to a plate of various meats, cheeses, and crackers on the table. Before Cora's coat and purse were even tucked away in Anna's bedroom though, Alex had already tossed down a couple of crackers and was now searching for a good-looking piece of salami.

"Alex!" Cora exclaimed. "Slow down honey! Matt and Lila aren't even here yet. You're messing up Anna's lovely food presentation!" She quickly walked over to him and took the salami out of his fingers. Alex's frown slowly turned to an amused smirk though, when he realized that Cora was going to eat the salami herself after wrapping it around a piece of cheese.

"Hey!" he shot back. "That was mine!" It was too late though, as Cora had already popped the tasty treat into her mouth and was giggling. Alex reached out to pull her towards him, the two of them now doubling over with laughter.

"Okay, okay you two love-birds," Anna said with a happy smile. "Knock it off or no wine for either of you!" she playfully teased. She watched as Cora took another piece of salami off the plate, only to have Alex snatch it away and quickly swallow it down. Then there was a knock at the front door, quickly followed by the appearance of Matt and Lila as it swung open.

Anna's friends knew that they could always just walk into her apartment if the door was unlocked. They also all had keys to her place, a contingency plan if Anna ever got locked out – which had already happened more than once, due to her ability to lose everything no matter how hard she tried. She actually loved feeling like her home was open to everyone she cared about, so it only made sense that they all had equal access. Of course, Alyssa had her own key as well, but she hadn't used it in a while. Anna felt a small pang in the middle of her heart as a knot began forming in her throat. For a moment, she felt guilty for having everyone over tonight.

What was Alyssa doing? Was she in the comfort of good friends at this same moment, or was she struggling to explain her next steps to their parents? Actions Anna didn't even know yet, because her sister wouldn't tell her…thinking of that made her mood shift slightly from sadness to frustration. It was enough to quickly push back any tears that had considered falling.

The tiny apartment got louder as Matt and Lila walked in and everyone scurried around them. The kind of energy that can only surround a group of the closest friends enveloped the room, and Anna soon felt safe in her decision to tell them about Collen. She knew it was the right thing to do, if she truly wanted it to work this time. Since she also knew that her friends didn't like Collen that much when they had first dated, and now even less after their break-up, she understood it would take some convincing to bring them onboard – but she was ready to do that…much more so than she had been when she and Alyssa had fought the other day.

Soon enough, everyone was settled with glasses of wine and a plate of appetizers. Anna knew it was time.

"So, I need to tell all of you something," she said slowly as she took another drink of her wine to try and calm the rapid beating of her heart. Just because she was ready to tell them, didn't mean she wasn't nervous as hell.

"Oh no…" Matt replied. "Please don't tell me you're really a dude. I could handle it, but I think Alex would be scarred for life!" Everyone in the room broke into laugher as Alex took his finger and marked the downward outline of an invisible tear running down his cheek. Anna was grateful that her friends were trying to make the situation humorous, but she was also now very worried that it meant the mood would quickly come crashing down. So, before she could stop herself, she heard the words spilling out of her mouth.

"It's actually about Collen."

Then…there was the silence she was anticipating.

"Collen?" Cora said in a confused voice. "*THE* Collen? Your Collen?" Obviously, Cora and Anna had talked a lot about Collen when she moved back, but this was the first time since she had dated Luke that his name had been spoken out loud again amongst their tight-knit group.

"He's not '*her Collen*' Cora," Alex quickly responded. "Anna kicked that guy to the curb years ago." He looked up at Anna with a look in his eyes that could only mean he definitely wasn't ready to hear what she was going to say next.

"Anna," Lila softly said. "What's going on?" She then reached out and grabbed Matt's hand, and it was then that Anna's heart sank. This was going to take much more than convincing.

"Oh god," Anna then whimpered as she put her face in her hands. "Please don't hate me you guys. I love you all so much. Please just promise me that you'll keep an open mind?" That last statement hung in the air for several seconds before Anna finally went on. There was no use putting it off any longer. Slowly…hesitantly…the words started tumbling awkwardly from her mouth.

"We're talking again," she almost whispered. She then exhaled loudly, as though the words had been choking the breath that was trying to escape from her lungs. Now that she had started though, her voice got louder and the rest came out quickly.

"I ran into him at the airport when I flew out for that conference a couple of weeks ago. At first, I couldn't believe it when I saw him in the security line – but the longer I waited, the more I knew I had to try and talk to him. So, I did. I finally got his attention, and I was so scared he wouldn't be happy to see me – but he was you guys! He really was! He's missed me all this time too. We've talked every day since then…and…well…he's coming to see me tomorrow."

There was an audible gasp from Cora after Anna said those last few words. She quickly started fumbling with the pendant hanging around her neck and looked uncomfortably at Alex. It pained Anna to see her struggling. Cora was the kindest among her friends, so she naturally would hold back if she thought even for a moment that she would upset anyone. Since Anna knew Cora wanted to say something, she tried to make it easier for her.

"Cora," Anna said softly. "It's okay. You can tell me what you're thinking. I know this came out of nowhere, but that's part of the reason I wanted to see you all tonight. You're my best friends and I don't want to keep anything from you."

Anna knew that last sentence was true, especially because of how badly things had backfired with Alyssa. If she had a choice, she may not have told her friends everything just yet. After the chaos of the last few days though, she knew that she had to put her newly revived relationship with Collen out in the open.

Secrets are for hiding something that a person can't come to terms with…but this was different. She wasn't sad anymore about what had happened between them before. She was hopeful now.

Cora looked away from Alex and straight into Anna's eyes.

"I'm just worried Anna," she finally replied sadly. "When things ended with Collen…well…it…" Cora was still searching for the right words.

Then, all of a sudden, there they were.

"It broke you."

Anna felt her stomach leap and she was instantly both nauseous and embarrassed all at once. She could feel intense warmth as the blood rushed to her face. She then quickly looked away, hoping her friends wouldn't see her turning a regretful shade of crimson. She knew Cora was right, but hearing it spoken out loud was a whole other story. It meant she had to face the reality of her situation back then, while simultaneously trying to escape from it so that she could embrace a new potential future with Collen. She didn't like how it felt, even for a brief handful of seconds.

Cora wasn't even close to being done though.

"It was like you had given up," she continued. "You were so depressed. Do you remember how you stopped eating? Alex and I had to beg you to take a couple of bites of anything after you lost too much weight. All you would do is sleep…we couldn't get you out of the apartment…" Cora was still talking, but Anna's thoughts had now retreated to when she first moved back. She was thinking of one day in particular. The day she had to finally make a choice.

She stood up and slowly walked to the living room window to look out on the deserted street below. Her friends were now mumbling to each other in the background, obviously worried, but unsure of what to do next.

It didn't matter to Anna though. She was back there now, in the dark.

CHAPTER SEVENTEEN

When Anna first moved back, she had to stay with Alex and Cora for a couple of weeks before she could move into her apartment. It turned out that Alyssa and Jess were in the middle of moving themselves, so she didn't want to complicate things further by being in the way. Having just moved halfway across the country herself, she also wasn't really in the mood for another round of filling up empty boxes. Fortunately for her, Alex and Cora were adamant that she stay with them and Anna knew it was good for her to have friends close by. Unfortunately, for them though, they saw her at the beginning of a drastic decline.

Sadly, what Cora had said was true. Anna had lost what she once was and felt tragically empty. She managed to make it through the first two weeks only because she wasn't completely alone. However, once she moved into her own place, things turned out to be much, much harder. Although she had obviously been depressed when she was at Alex and Cora's, the enormous impact of what had happened hit her in its entirety when she was on her own.

Her return to New Mexico had been sudden, so she didn't have a new job lined up yet and she was barely talking to anybody. The silence engulfing her every hour on the hour though, was not because her family and friends weren't trying to reach out. It was a side effect of purposefully turning off her cell phone the majority of the time, because she couldn't bear to look at it and know that Collen would not be on the other line any time she answered.

When she was honest with herself, Anna knew that truly was the hardest part of all. She couldn't hear his voice anymore. At one point, she did have one heart-wrenching voicemail he had left her shortly after they split, but she had quickly erased it after only listening a couple of times. He had obviously been drunk when he called, and in a rare moment of weakness, inebriated words were cast about as he selfishly admitted to missing her. He never once said that he wanted her to come back though, proving again to Anna that even with the strongest truth serum, Collen still saw things the same way.

To lose a best friend, a lover, a confidant…it opens up a part of someone that was once forever hidden and most definitely unfamiliar. The irony though, is that such a dark place is not meant to be explored, but instead is a black hole that slowly begins to pull a person down…down…down. After only a few days in her new apartment, the black hole had a firm grip on Anna.

On this particular day, she had dragged herself out of bed late in the morning and was soon standing in front of her open refrigerator. Even though it was packed with food that Alex and Cora had brought over a couple of days before, nothing looked appealing. These days, her mind was so consumed with Collen's absence that it had completely forgotten how to tell her body it was hungry. So, eating was not important to Anna anymore and it had only taken a month for this new reality to take hostage over her once curvy frame. She was oblivious to how loosely her clothes hung on her though, and didn't seem to mind the changes, as vanity and depression did not go hand in hand.

Anna slammed the refrigerator shut and slowly made her way to the couch. As she lay underneath the same blanket that had now become her only comfort in a self-made tomb, she closed her eyes and wished for a dreamless sleep – knowing it wouldn't come. Dreams were a certainty now, and they were always filled with images of Collen. She honestly hated herself for missing him so much, but still held on tightly to the fleeting feeling of his presence every time she slowly awakened. It was amazing how real he seemed in those moments…as though she would roll over and see him lying next to her, ready to reach out with both arms and gently pull her close to him.

She felt the tears starting and quickly turned on her back, just in time to feel the water fall down both cheeks and begin trickling behind her ears and neck.

"What is happening to me?" she desperately thought to herself. She pulled the blanket up and over her mouth, as though it could hold back the flood that was now coming, but it was too late. So, she did the only thing she could. She gave in again to the terrible sobbing that had taken her captive several times before. It jerked her body back and forth for so long, that her stomach began to cramp and ache, but that kind of pain she could handle. It was actually almost freeing, because she could feel something other than grief for once and it reminded her that she was still alive.

In a now muted part of her mind, Anna knew that she couldn't go on like this forever – but she was stuck in a hell that she didn't know how to return from and nothing else seemed normal anymore. This constant sadness though…it was her new normal and anyone that wanted to pull her away from it – well, they just didn't understand.

Or so she thought.

When she finally stopped crying, she opened her eyes and stared up at the ceiling. It was coated with that type of spackling that was supposed to look textured, but was instead soft and unstable. It always so easily broke away when she was trying to put up a hook, or if she had accidentally brushed up against it while changing a light bulb…little white pieces floating down from above, too small to cover anything, but plentiful enough to be a nuisance.

That was how Anna felt – soft, unstable, and too small for

anything.

She sensed herself sinking deeper into the couch, as if something was pushing her down. It felt heavy and dark, as it slowly washed over her entire body, but it didn't scare her. It was like a kind numbness, and Anna couldn't think of anything she wanted more in that moment.

She felt her eyes slowly start to close as the sensation continued to spread.

"Was this what it felt like to finally give up?"

Then, as she suddenly realized what was trying to overtake her, she heard the front door open.

It was Alyssa.

Anna watched from tired, swollen eyes as her sister quickly crossed the room and reached out with both arms.

Finally, someone really was reaching for her this time.

She pulled herself up and felt half of the blanket fall to the floor as Alyssa sat down and began to fiercely hug her.

"You can't do this anymore Anna," she firmly said as she softly rubbed her sister's back. Alyssa could feel her start shaking all over and began to hold her tighter. "This has gone on long enough. Don't give him this much power over you! You need to make a choice!"

She then pulled away from Anna and looked straight at her. "Is this going to be what you do every day from now on? Are you going to be a freaking mess for the next ten years? Are you going to be one of those women who never lets the past go and uses it as an excuse to be less than who she is? Because I'll tell you right now, there is no way I'm going to let that happen! So why should you?"

Anna stared back at her sister and suddenly felt lighter, as the heaviness that was there moments before started to slowly lift.

Even though her vision was distorted by a few remaining tears, she could finally see.

CHAPTER EIGHTEEN

Every day back then was a blur now…filled less with disjointed images, and instead, saturated by emotions that Anna could still feel trying to work back to the surface of her heart. Remembering that moment long ago when Alyssa yanked her away from a very real, and very near depression, just inspired Anna even more though to stay as far away from that past version of herself as possible.

Yes. Her eyes were wide open this time and she was ready for whatever lay ahead.

"Anna?" Cora's soft voice called to her in the background. "Anna?" she repeated in a panicked voice. "I'm so, so sorry. I shouldn't have said anything. You know that I love you right? I swear I'll stand by you, no matter what. You're smart and I have no doubt you've thought a lot about this."

Anna slowly turned away from the window and looked at her friends, who were now all standing huddled together. She immediately felt guilty for worrying them, but knew that she finally had the right words to say. The words that would make them understand.

"I know that when everything ended with Collen, I didn't handle it well," she started while slowly walking towards them. She then reached out and took Cora's hands in hers and looked around the room.

"I promise you right now though – that person is gone." She watched as a small smile started to appear on Lila's face, but Alex still looked hesitant at Matt. She wasn't worried though. There was still so much more to say.

"Losing Collen the first time was one of the hardest things I ever had to experience. I know now, more than ever though, that he was and still is the love of my life. Because you see…as wonderful as Luke was, he didn't have that kind of impact on me. The love I had for him wasn't *everything* to me. *He* wasn't everything to me. These last couple of weeks with Collen though…they've honestly meant more to me than all of the time I spent with Luke. I know that sounds a little harsh, but it's not because I'm brain-washed, or weak, or forgetting what happened in the past. It's actually because of that past that I want this second chance so much. Because don't you see? Yes, Collen almost broke me and I've never been the same since – but he's back now, and for the first time in years, I don't feel like something is missing anymore. I really do believe that there is a point to what we went through before, and that we can make that mean something now. This is our chance, not to erase the past, but to finally put it away completely."

As Anna finished that last sentence, she felt a lump form in her throat. Did her friends hear her? Did her words make any sense at all?

Cora finally let go of Anna's hands and hugged her hard. Anna felt a sense of relief wash over her, and then Lila came over to pull her into another hug.

"Please just promise me one thing," Lila cautiously said into Anna's ear. Anna nodded her head up and down in agreement, her arms still wrapped around her friend, knowing that she would do everything she could to keep a promise to Lila.

"Don't make Collen everything this time," she simply stated.

Anna released her hold on Lila and slowly stepped back with a confused look on her face.

"I don't understand," she then replied. Wasn't that was love was all about?

"When someone becomes your *everything*, it means they can leave you with nothing," Lila explained. "If this is really going to be different from last time, then don't let that happen again Anna. Okay? Take what you've learned in the past couple of years and do something you've never done before – be in love, but still be you."

Anna smiled at Lila and responded with two words.

"Of course," she said, even though she hadn't fully digested what Lila was trying to tell her. She reached out and hugged her again.

"Of course..."

CHAPTER NINETEEN

The day Collen arrived, he met Anna after work. She had planned to pick him up from the airport, but he had actually booked an earlier flight so that he could surprise her. She had no idea he would be there as she walked as fast as possible away from the beige stucco university buildings towards the parking garage. Her heart began racing in anticipation as she got closer and could see the outline of the back of her SUV, the front still hidden amongst a line of different-colored cars. Then, it suddenly stopped completely when she realized that he was already there.

He had pulled his rental car into a parking space a few feet from hers and was waiting with the driver's side door open. She saw him sitting halfway inside and turned slightly sideways, with his left leg placed firmly on the concrete. Anna had spotted him first, so she had only a brief couple of seconds to compose herself. It would be hard. She watched as the light from the screen of his cell phone turned off and he put it on the passenger's seat. Quickly, her face began to feel hot as she felt her entire body instantly captivated by his every movement.

There was no doubt that he had become even more attractive during their years apart. How that was even possible, she didn't know. Perhaps, it's what inevitably happens when people reach their goals one by one and gradually become content and confident in who they are – although, confidence was never something Collen lacked. When they were together, Anna quickly appreciated that even though he wasn't a natural at everything he did, he still had an ability to look like he was. He also had the rare gift of making anybody feel special in his presence…as she was reminded of now, while finally standing only a few feet away from him again for the second time in what had felt like forever.

Collen's dark features were silhouetted by the fading light of the day, making him seem almost like an etching in an artist's notepad. Anna felt her heart speeding up again, as she considered saying something, but then he looked over and saw her waiting. In an instant, his brown eyes ignited and a gorgeous smile spread across his face. This was it…he was finally here for her.

She sensed a slight hesitation before he stood up and took his first step towards her, and it was in that moment that she realized he must be as nervous as she was. It calmed her almost instantly though, and she began walking towards him as well. The distance between them was small enough to cover in seconds, but Anna still felt like if she didn't walk fast enough, he would disappear – proving to her that this really was all a dream. She watched as he opened his arms wide, inviting her towards him with an expression on his face that could only come from a man who was finally ready to let go of regrets. So, before she could even take one more breath, Anna fell completely into him…his muscular body now engulfing her small frame. She could feel his heart beating against her chest so strongly, it was as though it would burst through and give itself up to her forever. Soon, its rapid pulsing was matched by the one pounding inside her, and all at once she felt overcome with desire for him.

Before anything more could happen, she found the strength to pull out of his embrace and look straight into his eyes. Collen was smiling down on her, as he took his right hand and gently brushed a piece of hair away from her face.

"God, I've missed you Anna. I never thought I'd feel this way again," he softly said to her, before placing his lips on her forehead…then her cheek…and finally her neck. Anna felt the fire ignite inside her and she leaned into him again.

"Neither did I," she whispered in his ear. She then quickly threw her arms around his neck again and felt him pull her light body upwards into his steady, sculpted arms. They held onto each other for a few more seconds until it was impossible to hold back any longer. Suddenly, his lips were firmly on her mouth, kissing her over and over again. He was remarkably gentle and intense all at the same time. Anna could barely remember where they were as she felt his hands move up to cup her face. As much as she had held onto him all this time, she had buried what this felt like…everything was spinning, and yet, nothing was out of focus.

Unfortunately, the sudden start of a car motor quickly brought them out of the moment.

"Oh!" Anna said in a startled voice. Collen's arms wrapped themselves around her again as her body reacted to the abrupt noise. She was shaking now, but couldn't be sure if it was because of their passionate reunion or the unfortunate interruption.

"You okay baby?" he murmured while still holding steadily onto her.

"Mmmmm…" Anna responded sweetly, feeling herself swaying softly back and forth. "Yes…I'm perfect."

"You're telling me," Collen quipped back, causing Anna to giggle.

"Stop it!" she teased. "We're still in the middle of a parking garage."

"Well," Collen then said in an all too familiar voice. "How about we fix that?"

Thirty minutes later, they were checked into his hotel room.

Anna stood at the large, glass window and watched as the sun began to set. Orange, red, and purple ribbons of light reflected off her dark brown eyes and filled the sky with a color so radiant, it almost seemed painted by something not of this world.

"It's beautiful," Collen softly said, as he came up beside her and placed his right arm tenderly around her shoulder. Anna tilted her head so that it was resting against him, and felt the final surge of emotions begin to seep out from the last hidden places of her heart. Standing here with Collen…the only man who had ever made her feel both helpless and hopeful at the same time…it felt so right, that she couldn't help but think it was worth losing herself for a while.

So…as she felt his fingers begin to move over her body, everything relaxed and she knew then that there was nowhere else she would rather be than right here…with him…bathed in fiery, blinding light.

CHAPTER TWENTY

That first night, the two reacquainted lovers never left Collen's hotel room. Instead, they made the most of being back in each other's arms and lying together in the same bed. They barely slept, as they tried to use every moment possible to quench the desire that had been building between them again for almost a month. Anna knew she hadn't felt this alive since before they broke up, and although she was grateful to have the man she loved by her side again, it also scared her.

She already knew what it felt like to lose him once, and she didn't know if she could handle that kind of empty misery again.

As they lay together, wrapped in each other's arms, the fear started to consume her. Anna felt her body tighten in response and suddenly, she was cold in the very warm bed. Collen noticed the change right away and instantly slid closer to her.

"What's wrong?" he softly asked her.

Anna stayed silent for a few seconds, as she tried to form the words that could adequately describe all of the emotions spinning in her mind. It almost seemed cruel to bring up the subject now, after they had just spent hours molded together in the moonlight – but, she didn't want to lie to him. There was no room for secrets between them, after they'd come this far.

"I guess…" Anna started slowly. "I guess, I'm just a little bit worried."

Collen didn't say a word, allowing her to continue at her own pace. Instead, he made sure to let her know he was listening, by slowly running the fingers of his right hand up and down her bare arm.

"You and I are back together Collen." A slight shake could be heard in Anna's voice and she could feel her throat trying to close up on her, but she went on. "I mean, I honestly never thought that would happen for us. I've spent years trying to get over you, and now here we are again. What does it all mean? Will it be okay this time?"

There was no way to hide the tears that had quickly appeared. Anna pulled the sheet upwards to try and conceal them, but instead, Collen turned her around so that she was facing him. He took his hand and gently wiped the moisture away that was glistening on her face.

"Anna," he responded. "I want you to hear me very carefully, okay?"

Her heart was pounding so loudly, Anna swore he could hear it. She moved her head up and down to signal to him that he had her full attention.

"I think you and I both know that life is full of uncertainties. I wish I could tell you that this is going to work out, but I can't do that. It wouldn't be fair to you."

Anna felt her stomach start to twist upon itself, and suddenly all she could think about was that day in their old apartment years ago. It was their last day together "pretending", and he changed everything by finally telling her he couldn't understand why she would ever forgive him. It was then that she saw the truth. He couldn't stay with her because he didn't respect her.

Did he respect her now? She had to know.

"Do you still think I'm weak?" she quietly asked.

"What?" Collen responded in a startled voice. "When have I ever called you weak?" He didn't sound angry, but he did pull slightly away from her. She resisted the urge to fill the slight space between them and sat up instead.

"It wasn't that you said those exact words," Anna answered sadly. "When everything was a mess right before I moved out though, you said that no matter what you did, I would always forgive you – and you implied that you couldn't love me because of that."

"No, Anna…no…" Collen quickly sat up now too. "That's totally not what I meant. To be honest, I don't even know what I was thinking back then! You and I both know I wasn't in a good place. I do know that I hate the way I treated you though. I was an idiot! Please, let's just forget that entire conversation ever happened. I could never see you as weak. Never."

"*Forget that conversation?*" Anna thought to herself. How was that even possible? That conversation…those words…she must have replayed them in her mind at least a thousand times.

"Collen…" Anna started to say, but she wasn't going to get the chance to finish her sentence.

"Anna, please!" Collen replied firmly, as he put his hands on her shoulders and tried to turn her body towards him. "Let's stop talking about this. It's such a waste of time! We just had an amazing night together. Why do you want to ruin that? Why does what happened years ago even matter? We're together now, right?"

Anna looked in Collen's eyes as he said that last sentence and she physically felt the struggle going on between her mind and her heart, but instead of pushing the topic further, she decided that Collen was right. They weren't the same people from back then, so of course this new relationship wouldn't be the same either. Or at least, she hoped it wouldn't be the same. She put her arms around him and felt his bare chest against hers. They both fell together on the bed, and any lingering thoughts about the past instantly retreated.

Everything was in slow motion now, as they began to make love again….but this time, it felt different. Anna was fully aware of every touch, every movement, and every audible gasp between them. It was as though all her senses were heightened. She felt invigorated and overwhelmed all at once. She felt beautiful…and in a strange way, she felt free.

Afterwards, she put her head on his chest and tried to catch her breath – but it was too soon for that, as Anna was about to hear the one thing she never thought she'd hear from Collen ever again.

"I love you," he tenderly whispered as he moved his fingers through her hair. To Anna though, it was as though he had shouted the words.

Suddenly, she knew that whatever happened this time, she was going to have to come out of it more than she was now. Exactly what that meant though…well, she wasn't sure.

Not just yet.

CHAPTER TWENTY-ONE

Anna and Collen were inseparable all weekend. When they weren't at the hotel, they spent their time together revisiting a couple of their favorite places and driving around the city. It was too easy to reminisce, and so they fell into a familiar pattern where it almost seemed as though they had never left in the first place. DC had never happened. No one had ever been hurt.

They had always had each other.

When it came time to be responsible again, they both grudgingly went to work. At first, Anna found it hard to focus, electrified by the fact that she would be meeting up with Collen again in the evening. The building site was only a few miles away from the college too. So, it was even more difficult to know that he was just a handful of minutes away – rather than a three hour plane ride. She quickly realized though that they were quite good at sending out flirtatious text messages to each other all day, which obviously helped build up the anticipation of being in each other's arms again.

After the first week had passed, Anna finally heard from Alyssa. Although she had obviously been distracted, her sister had not been far from her mind, so she was more than eager to talk. The conversation was quick, but meaningful.

She had been packing an overnight bag so that she could meet up with Collen at the hotel when her cell phone rang. As soon as she saw her sister's picture light up the screen, she desperately reached out for her phone. In her clumsiness though, it fell to the ground next to a pile of discarded clothes. As Anna dropped to the floor, she frantically started searching all around her. She could still hear the continual ringing of the popular hip-hop song that was Alyssa's ringtone, but it sounded quieter now. Finally, as she reached under the bed, her fingers brushed up against the hard, plastic case the salesperson at the store had convinced her into buying. It had already proven helpful, as this sadly had to be the thousandth time Anna had dropped her phone. She quickly pulled it out and tapped on the screen to answer her sister's call.

"Hello? Alyssa? Are you okay?" The words came out a little too abruptly, but Anna couldn't help it. She had finally gotten to a point where she missed her sister so much, that she didn't care if a conversation meant getting into a fight. She just wanted to hear her voice again.

"I'm fine," Alyssa replied in a soft voice. "How about you?"

"I'm great!" Anna quickly responded. She then realized that she sounded a little too happy, considering the monumental fight they had gotten into and the fact that Alyssa was out of town trying to figure things out.

"I mean..." she continued in a less frenzied voice. "I'm great now that I've heard from you! I've been worried about you. Are you coming home soon?" Anna's heart was beating hard and fast, filled with a love that only a sister could bring forth.

"Actually," Alyssa started. "That's why I'm calling. I'm coming back next week. I was hoping we could meet up."

"Of course!" Anna yelled out. "I'd love to see you! I've missed you!" Even with Collen in town, this was exactly what she'd been hoping her sister would say. She waited a few seconds and then slowly felt her stomach begin to twist up as the other end of the line stayed silent. It worried her that

Alyssa might still be really angry. They had never been in a fight this long. Anna couldn't help but hate herself in the moment for even letting this happen. Then, she heard the muffled crying sound.

"Alyssa?" she hesitantly asked. "Alyssa? What's wrong?"

The crying continued, but now Alyssa's voice finally broke through.

"Nothing's wrong sister." Her voice was cracking, but Anna could hear the sincerity in her words. "I've just missed you too. A lot…"

That's all it took for the tears to quickly well up in Anna's eyes.

"I'm so sorry about everything Alyssa." Anna was now quickly pacing around the room, trying to remember the apology that she'd been crafting in her head for days. "I never meant for things to get so crazy! I really do wish now that I had talked to you. I just didn't know what to say. Does that make any sense?" Anna was almost sobbing now, and before she could help herself, even more truth spilled out.

"I honestly still can't believe he's back sometimes either."

This was it. She had been completely honest and didn't hide that Collen was in fact truly back in her life. She braced herself for the consequences and lay down on the floor to look up at the ceiling. It was a view that she was all too familiar with, considering she had spent so much time staring at it after everything had gone down.

Suddenly, Anna felt a strong sense of doubt start to come over her. It surprised her so quickly, that she shot back up so that she was sitting upright again. Before she could even stop to consider what the hell had just happened though, Alyssa finally said something.

"We don't have to talk about that Anna. I know that you and I see things differently, and I really don't want to fight about it anymore. I think now, more than ever, we should just let the whole thing go." That last sentence struck Anna. What did her sister mean? *Now, more than ever?*

"You sound weird," Anna responded awkwardly. "Are you

sure we shouldn't talk more about what happened?" Even though she was scared about what her sister might say, she wanted to face the situation head on this time.

"No," Alyssa said quickly. "It's fine. I promise. Anyway, we can talk more when I'm back in town."

Anna wasn't comfortable with the turn their conversation had taken, but she decided not to press the issue. Instead, the sisters made plans to meet up for lunch when Alyssa got back in a few days and they hung up.

That night, while she and Collen were eating dinner in his hotel room, Anna was still replaying the conversation with Alyssa in her mind. She had been pushing her pasta around with her fork for a couple of minutes when he finally said something.

"You seem distracted." Collen's voice was gentle as he reached out and took the fork out of her hand. He laid it on her plate and then lifted her chin up so that Anna's eyes were staring straight at his. "What's wrong?" he asked hesitantly, concern written all over his face.

"Is it me?"

Anna's heart sank as his words slammed against her heart and she instantly felt selfish for worrying him.

"No!" she responded immediately. "I promise! I'm so sorry for making you even think that!" She reached out and put his hands in hers. "It's not you at all. I hope you can see that."

Collen's shoulders relaxed a little and Anna strangely felt comforted knowing that for a few moments he was actually worried. For her, it solidified that they were on the same page and neither one of them wanted things to go back to the way they were.

"It's my sister," she quietly said.

A flash of emotion seemed to move across Collen's face. Anna could have sworn it was annoyance, but it happened so quickly, that she wasn't sure. Before she could even ask a question though, he was saying something.

"So, what's going on then?" He had pulled away and gone back to his meal at this point, slowing cutting a piece of ravioli in half and lifting it to his mouth. Anna felt the blood flowing to her face, remembering all too easily how Collen acted when something was bothering him.

"Ummm…" she responded in a somewhat confused voice. "Do you really want to know? Because it seems like you don't." She couldn't believe that she was actually going to be confrontational, but it was impossible to avoid. Her past experience with his moody nature was coming back to the surface, and Anna couldn't help but think she hadn't done anything wrong.

Collen took a bite of the remaining ravioli half and then wiped his mouth with the cloth napkin that had been sitting in his lap.

"Of course I want to know," he said in a slightly exasperated voice. "Even though we're supposed to be having a romantic dinner, I do want to know what the problem is with your sister." He started fumbling with the napkin again, folding it along the crease lines already present in the cloth.

"Why do you sound like that?" Anna responded sadly. "It's not like I was trying to ruin dinner. I'm just worried about her." She wanted to stop talking, but now that her concerns had been voiced out loud, it was too hard. "I talked to her today and she wasn't herself. I think she's still upset about everything that happened."

It was then that Anna suddenly remembered that she hadn't told him about the fight. In fact, she had purposefully avoided it. They had talked about a lot of things the past few days, and in all the late night phone conversations leading up to this trip, but not about the people in their lives.

Not about co-workers.

Not about friends.

Not about her sister.

"Everything that happened?" Collen asked. "What are you talking about? What happened?" An honest look of bewilderment was on his face.

"Well…" she started hesitantly. "We kind of got into a fight."

"A fight? About what?"

Unlike Anna, Collen's voice was not hesitant. In fact, it sounded almost a little harsh. Her mind was spinning, trying to figure out another angle…another approach…anything that wouldn't make him feel like a bad guy – but there was no point. She had brought the topic up in the first place. Maybe it was finally time to bring him up to speed.

"About you," Anna finally responded in a dejected tone. "The fight was about you."

CHAPTER TWENTY-TWO

Alyssa and Collen had never gotten along. Unlike Anna's friends who had kept their concerns quietly to themselves, Alyssa had voiced early on in the relationship that she did not approve of Collen for her sister.

The first time it had come up, was after Anna had both of them over for dinner. Alyssa had only been in Albuquerque for a few months, as it was her first year of college. She had briefly met Collen once before, during a party at Alex and Cora's, but they obviously didn't get any time alone to talk. Anna was hoping that this dinner would naturally bring them together, but after only about fifteen minutes in, she quickly realized that wasn't going to happen.

Ironically, everything had started off nicely. Anna had tried to set a light-hearted atmosphere for the meal, by not getting too fancy. So, instead of making something out of one of the cookbooks she had bought after she started dating Collen – he was a true foodie – she opted to make her mom's famous steak and potato soup instead. She had even found the perfect loaf of sourdough bread in the grocery store bakery earlier that day, and couldn't wait to break it open and soak up the fragrant, warm tomato and herb broth.

As everyone filled their bowls with ladles of hot soup and

walked towards the small table to settle into their seats, Collen started asking Alyssa about herself.

"So, Anna tells me that you just got a job at a dog grooming place," he said friendly enough.

"Yup!" Alyssa said happily. "I start on Monday. Obviously, I'm going to be the low man on the totem pole at first, but I'm hoping they'll teach me how to actually groom the dogs after I've proven myself."

"That's cool," Collen responded. "So, you'll just be cleaning up and doing grunt work? Checking people in? Washing floors? Running errands? That kind of thing?"

"Probably," Alyssa replied thoughtfully. "I don't have any grooming experience, so I doubt they'll let me do more than that for a while. I'm super lucky to have gotten the job in the first place."

"How did you hear about it?" Collen asked.

"Oh!" Alyssa exclaimed. "You don't know? It's all because of Anna! She's awesome! She found it for me. I guess a friend of hers knows the owner."

Collen gave Anna a curious look.

"Lila went to high school with the owner's daughter," she replied sweetly. "They're still really close. When I mentioned that Alyssa was looking for a job, she told me they were hiring and we should check it out. She knows how much Alyssa loves dogs."

"Well, isn't that something?" Collen said as he pursed his lips together and pensively nodded his head up and down. "It's not often that jobs just fall into your lap. Hmmph…" He reached towards his beer and took a slow drink. At the same time, Anna noticed a slight look of irritation quickly pass over her sister's face and felt her stomach jump. There was nothing to worry about just yet though.

"You're totally right," Alyssa then firmly said. "It wouldn't have happened without Anna. I definitely owe her one." She picked up her soup spoon and used it to start stirring her food around. She usually had a really good appetite. Anna was surprised she hadn't taken a single bite yet.

"It's good that you realize that," Collen replied. "A lot of kids take that kind of thing for granted. You know?"

"*Kids?*" Anna thought to herself. She couldn't help but wonder if she was thinking too much of it, but that word just seemed a little condescending – being that Alyssa was nineteen. Her sister didn't say a word though, so Anna decided to take her lead and quickly put a spoonful of soup in her mouth. She instantly felt the hot liquid scorch her tongue and all of the surrounding tissue.

"Damn it!" Anna exclaimed, as she suddenly dropped the spoon and put her napkin to her face to try and hide her visible embarrassment.

"What's wrong?" Alyssa worriedly asked at the same time as Collen swiftly said, "Baby, what happened?"

"I'm sorry! I'm sorry!" she quickly responded. "I just burned myself." She got up, immediately walked towards the sink, and poured herself a cold glass of water. Alyssa gave Collen a concerned look, but he just shrugged his shoulders. Her eyes narrowed and she opened her mouth to say something, but Anna jumped in before anything came out. "I'm okay! Really. I promise. I guess I was just paying more attention to the conversation than my food. I'm sorry you guys." She walked back to her seat and slowly sat down. Alyssa snuck a glance at her, but Anna was smiling apologetically at Collen. He gave her a quick grin before taking another drink of his beer.

"So," he was now staring directly at Alyssa, who was looking a little uncomfortable in her chair, "I'm assuming you don't want to be a dog groomer for the rest of your life. Tell me your plans. What do you want to major in?"

"Honestly," Alyssa said a little cautiously, "I'm not sure yet. I know what I like…animals, reading, going to plays. I'm just not sure how any of that translates into a career yet though. I'm assuming I have some time to figure it out."

"Not really," Collen replied. "You really don't want to be taking a bunch of introductory classes that you eventually won't need. The sooner you figure it out, the better."

"Collen," Anna spoke up, "It's only her first year. I didn't declare a major until I was a sophomore. She's fine." Anna knew that it was hard for Alyssa to open up to new people. She was amazed the conversation about school had even gotten this far. Normally, her sister would have kept her responses pretty basic. She knew she was trying.

"I promise I'm thinking about it," Alyssa responded to both of them. "It's just so complicated. How am I supposed to know that what I choose now is what I'm still going to want to do years from now?"

"Good point," Collen responded. He took a drink of his beer and then went on. "You're basically only a tenth of the person you're going to end up being in a few years. You honestly don't know anything yet, but you could at least pick a major. Even if you go into a different field later on, having a degree will help open some doors."

Anna couldn't help but stare at him in horror. Did he really just say that? She knew Collen was trying to be helpful, but it was coming across all wrong. For someone that could be so eloquent, he was sounding kind of rude. She hesitantly looked over at Alyssa to try and get some sort of indication of what she was thinking, and watched her take in a long, slow breath. As Anna began to brace herself for what she now thought was unavoidable, Alyssa instead gently used the air in her lungs to carefully blow on the liquid in her spoon. She kept her eyes down, as she finally responded to Collen's comment.

"That's true," she said carefully. "I totally get that I still have a few things to learn." Her eyes were still on her bowl, as she dumped back in what was on her spoon so that she could use it to slowly start moving a piece of potato from side to side.

Anna felt the worry starting to grow inside her, but decided to try and be positive – for everyone's sake.

"Isn't it crazy how much a couple of years can make all the difference?" she kindly responded. "I can only imagine what lessons are still waiting around the corner for me!" She knew that second sentence sounded a little too "rah-rah", and somewhat lame, but it did get Alyssa to look up and give her a small smile. "Remember how long it took for me to figure out that I wanted to teach?" she went on attentively. "It kind of snuck up on me."

"Yeah," her sister started. "I definitely have a ways to go when it comes to school…I kind of always thought I would know what I wanted to do right away. It's been weird to be so confused." She leaned back in her chair and looked thoughtfully at Anna. "But, I guess that's a good thing – right? It means I'm not settling." The smile was now growing a little bigger on her face, evidence that she had seen the other side of the coin and was going to let Collen's previous statement go. Anna felt relief start to flood through her as she relaxed and watched Alyssa finally reach over to grab a piece of bread from the center of the table.

"My classes are already proving to be nuts too," Alyssa continued. "I have so much homework and reading to do! It's totally not what I expected. But, I would be lying if I said I wasn't enjoying it. It's actually been a lot of fun so far!" She then finally dipped into her food, eagerly taking a bite of the bread and instantly moaning with ravenous pleasure. "Oh Anna! This is delicious! Too bad Jess couldn't make it."

"We'll invite him next time for sure," Anna said easily. She was grateful that the topic of conversation had smoothly transitioned towards something less tenuous – or so she thought.

"Definitely," Alyssa replied appreciatively, as she gave her sister a genuine smile.

"So, tell me about this Jess guy," Collen said inquisitively. "Did you meet him here?"

"We actually met in high school," Alyssa responded. "We started dating our senior year. When I got into college after we graduated, he decided to come with me."

"And what does he want to do? Please don't tell me he wants to start a band or something," Collen sarcastically retorted as he finished off the last of his beer.

"Actually…he doesn't know yet either," Alyssa replied

firmly. Anna could tell she was becoming defensive now, as her relationship was definitely not something up for criticism. School was one thing, but Jess was completely different. "But, you know what?" she continued, "I'm not worried about it. He'll probably figure it out before I do."

"I hope so," Collen chuckled. "Who knows? It'll probably happen around the same time you two break up."

That was all it took for dinner to head drastically off course.

Anna sharply turned to him, her eyes wide, trying to send silent thoughts his way.

What was he thinking?!?!?

Apparently, Collen wasn't done though and was setting the stage for an even more offensive comment.

"And what is that supposed to mean?" Alyssa asked stonily.

"Really?" Collen replied in a somewhat surprised voice. "Well, I hate to say it, but I'd be surprised if that boyfriend of yours doesn't move on in the next six months. A guy shouldn't settle on just one girl at his age. He needs to sleep with at least a few more people before he really knows what he wants."

Anna watched as heat poured into Alyssa's cheeks. She put her spoon down and carefully cleared her throat.

"Wow," Alyssa responded coolly, the optimistic attitude from a minute before now gone. "That didn't sound horrible at all." The serious look on her face spoke volumes, leaving no room for doubt that she was definitely pissed off.

"Are you serious?" Collen quipped back, his right eyebrow raised slightly as he looked at Alyssa. "You know I'm right," he then said matter-of-factly. "It's what I would do anyway."

Anna felt herself slowly sink into her chair, her heart pounding in her chest.

"Oh, really?" Alyssa replied. "Is that what you're going to do to my sister? Or is that what you've already done to some other girl? Either way, both would make you a pretty selfish human being." In an attempt to emphasize her point, Alyssa was now glaring at Collen with her arms crossed against her chest. That was one thing Anna admired about her. She was never afraid to speak her mind. Although now, Anna was silently wishing that wasn't always the case.

"You guys…" Anna started to say slowly, but her words were quickly drowned out by Collen.

"Oh, here we go…" he said with a slight smirk on his face. "I'm the dick. I'm the one who is actually going to tell you what men really think and do, but that makes me the bad guy. This is exactly what I was getting at when I mentioned his age. That little boyfriend of yours may be into you now, but it's not going to last. There are too many good-looking girls in this town and he's going to get bored soon enough."

"Collen!" Anna responded in disbelief. He looked at her, but instead of seeing understanding in his eyes, Anna watched as he shrugged his shoulders and then looked back at her sister.

"Are you kidding me?!" Alyssa shot back, jumping out of her chair. "Who the hell are you to tell me anything about my boyfriend? You don't know him or me at all! How dare you act like him cheating on me is just a fact of life! Who even says that? Do you know how that makes you sound? Doesn't it worry you at all that you're saying any of this in front of my sister?"

"The fact that I'm dating your sister has nothing to do with this conversation," Collen responded in an even tone. "She is an adult and knows that our relationship is different."

"It has everything to do with this conversation!" Alyssa shouted. "You may think you're better than me because I'm a stupid little nineteen-year-old girl, but at least I'm not a jerk! I know how to treat people!"

Anna watched as her sister stormed out of the kitchen and walked quickly towards the back bedroom. She knew Alyssa was fighting back angry tears and that she didn't want Collen to see how much he'd gotten to her. If Anna had been smart, she would have prepared herself for this reality the second the conversation started going badly. She should have foreseen that both her sister and her new boyfriend were the last two people on the planet who would ever back down from an argument.

She turned to look at Collen who didn't look distressed at all about what had just happened.

"What's wrong with you?" Anna asked in a disappointed voice. "Why would you say that to her?"

"Because it's the truth," Collen replied easily.

"Collen!" Anna responded desperately. "She's my sister! You totally offended her!"

"Oh, she'll get over it. I think you're worrying about nothing. I did her a favor by being honest."

"A favor? You just met her. Don't you think her opinion of you matters?" Anna looked back down the hall towards the bedroom, wondering if Alyssa was getting even more enraged by the minute.

"Anna," Collen said, as he got up from the table and started walking towards her. "My only concern is you. Not Alyssa. I shouldn't have to change my opinions just to get her approval. It's not like this is a three-person relationship. She is also totally blowing everything out of proportion. Such drama – just another side effect of being too young for a serious relationship." He seemed quite proud of his observations, as he pulled Anna in for a hug. She had to admit, he was making some good points – although, they were slightly obnoxious.

Actually, she wondered to herself, why wasn't *she* more upset? She obviously didn't like what had happened or what Collen had said, and normally, she would have followed right after Alyssa.

"Will you go with me to talk to her? Please?" Anna pleaded. She couldn't help but think that he had been a little dramatic too, and that he really didn't mean everything he had just said. Sometimes, he just couldn't avoid a good argument.

Collen smiled down at her and brushed a piece of hair away from her face. Anna felt her reserve continue to melt away.

"Yes, baby…" he responded. "I'll go with you."

"And will you say you're sorry?" Anna asked, even though she knew the chances were slim that Alyssa would accept an apology.

"Fine," Collen said, as he kissed her on the cheek. "I can do that. For you."

Anna smiled softly at him and took his hand as they walked together towards the bedroom. She was positive now that he hadn't meant what he'd said. A few seconds later, they were standing at the door.

"Alyssa?" she called out as she knocked softly. "We're coming in, okay?"

There was no response, so Anna started to turn the door knob. She cracked the door open slightly and looked in the room. Alyssa was lying on the bed, her face hidden in a pillow.

"Alyssa? Are you okay?" Such a stupid question to ask, but someone had to say something. The tension was all around them and Collen wasn't offering up any apologies yet.

"No!" Alyssa shouted back strongly, as she sat up on the bed. "I'm not okay! And I don't want to talk to HIM!" She pointed directly at Collen, who just slightly chuckled.

"Alyssa," he said calmly. "Don't you think you're being a little silly?"

"*Nice apology*," Anna thought to herself.

"Get out of here!" Alyssa responded angrily. "You don't know anything!" She then turned to Anna. "How are you okay with this? He's being mean and you're not even doing anything!" More tears started streaming down her face.

"Alyssa," Anna said quietly, hoping her tone would help soothe her sister. "He didn't mean anything by it. I promise." She sat on the bed next to Alyssa and was just about to hug her when another burst of emotion exploded from her sister.

"If you're crazy enough to defend him after what he said to me, then that's fine!" Alyssa cried out as she leaped off the bed, roughly wiping the tears off her face with the sleeve of her sweatshirt.

"I'm not defending him!" Anna quickly replied. "I just think this whole thing blew up out of nowhere. Collen wasn't trying to make you mad."

"Alyssa," Collen suddenly said. "I'm sorry. Anna's right. I

wasn't trying to make you mad." He had positioned himself in the middle of the room, in between Anna and Alyssa.

"*Finally!*" Anna exclaimed to herself.

"I just thought you'd want to hear the truth," he then continued nonchalantly.

Anna knew instantly that sentence was going to be the final nail in the coffin.

"Whatever!" Alyssa shot back coldly towards Collen. Anna watched in amazement as her sister instantly went calm though, her eyes bright with resentment now, instead of tears. "I don't believe you," she then said firmly. "You don't know everything about men, and you know why? Because you aren't anything close to a man. In fact, you've just proven to me tonight that you are far from it."

Anna watched as Collen's face hardened, his mouth set in a firm line. He suddenly had nothing left to say.

"You know what Collen?" Alyssa continued in a cruel voice, "My sister might like you, but I don't have to. I know who you are." She then abruptly turned around and walked out of the room.

"Wait!" Anna exclaimed. "Alyssa? Where are you going?"

"I'm going home," Alyssa called back over her shoulder. "I'm not hungry anymore. You guys can finish dinner without me."

Anna quickly got off the bed and followed her sister to the living room, where she quietly gathered her things and then promptly walked out the door.

"I'll be right back," Anna said to Collen, her eyes not looking at him, but at the space where her sister was just seconds before.

"Just let her go Anna," he quickly replied in an aggravated voice. "We'll have a much more enjoyable evening without her. Believe me."

"Are you serious right now?" Anna said sadly as she turned towards him. "I can't let her leave like this." She quickly exited the living room and ran outside.

"Alyssa!" she yelled towards her sister, who was already

halfway in her car. "Stop!"

Alyssa sighed and stepped back out onto the street.

"What?" she yelled back harshly.

"What the heck just happened in there?" Anna asked. "Why did you get so upset?"

"He's a creep Anna," Alyssa spat back. "I honestly don't know what you see in him."

"Okay…" Anna started. "I know he didn't make the best impression, but he's not a creep. He is somewhat opinionated, and that might come out wrong at times, but he thought he was being helpful. He really wasn't trying to tick you off."

"Well he did," Alyssa said plainly.

"Well, he's sorry!" Anna firmly replied.

"No he's not! He just said that so he'd get sex tonight. He doesn't give a crap about what I think." Alyssa started getting back into her car, as Anna stared at her in shock. "It won't last you know. He only cares about himself."

"Alyssa! How can you say that? Now who's being mean?" Anna called at her through the car window.

"I have a right to be mean to you! I'm your sister and I'm telling you the truth! But, that's fine. Do what you want. Just do me a favor and don't invite me over to hang out with him again anytime soon." Alyssa then turned her key in the ignition, but she had one more thing to say before driving away.

"Be careful Anna," she said seriously as she looked straight into her sister's eyes. "You're too nice. This guy will take advantage of that."

Anna sadly stared back at Alyssa. "You just need more time to get to know him," she finally said.

"Nope," Alyssa said. "I think I've seen enough."

Anna watched her drive away and then looked over at her apartment. Collen was standing in the open doorway, light shining from the room behind him, but his face was lost in the shadows.

"Babe," he called out to Anna. "She's going to be fine. I already told you. Let's finish eating."

Anna slowly walked towards his voice, but she couldn't get

her sister's words out of her head. Soon, they were both sitting back at the table in the kitchen.

"You know," Collen said happily. "This bread is delicious!" He dipped it into his bowl, took a big bite, and then smiled at Anna. It was obvious he was much more content with her sister gone – the past few minutes now a distant memory.

She weakly smiled back and then stared long and hard at her food, wishing for a do-over, but knowing it was impossible.

Alyssa never spent time alone with either of them together again.

CHAPTER TWENTY-THREE

As Anna looked at Collen from across the table, she decided that there was too much antagonistic history between him and her sister. Rehashing the fight her and Alyssa had was not going to help anything, and she certainly didn't want him to know that he'd been right about Jess. They had been trying to keep the past in the past, and this was just another opportunity to do that. So, she decided to keep the details brief.

"You got into a fight about me?" he asked. "Let me guess. She's mad that I'm back in your life." Anna could hear the irritation growing with each word he spoke and knew she had to act quickly.

"Honestly," she softly said. "It's all my fault." She got up from her chair and moved so that she was standing behind him. As she leaned down, she wrapped her arms around his shoulders and spoke gently, her face against the side of his right cheek. "I handled everything wrong. Alyssa has a lot going on right now. She just broke up with someone and has been really emotional. Then I made things worse by keeping our new relationship to myself. So, when I finally told her that we were talking again, she felt left out."

There. That didn't sound so bad. Right?

"Oh..." Collen replied slowly. "So, can I ask you this?" He moved her so that Anna was no longer behind him, but now sitting on his lap. "Why didn't you tell her about me?" His voice wasn't accusatory, but sad. The sound alone sent a small crack through her heart.

"It wasn't because I was ashamed," Anna responded lovingly. She put her hand on his cheek and let her fingers gently glide down his face. "Is that what you're thinking?"

Collen looked at her with those gorgeous brown eyes and all she could feel was adoration. He then took her hand in his and started playing with her fingers.

"I just want us to have our chance. I'm afraid that won't happen if you think you need everyone else's approval."

Approval. Anna found it interesting to hear that word again in the context of a conversation about her sister.

"I don't need everyone's approval Collen," Anna replied carefully, "but if we do want things to be different this time, then maybe that could include your relationship with my sister?" She leaned slightly forward and placed one small kiss on his cheek...sweetly, deliberately, but almost seductively.

"Maybe," he said uncertainly. "But, we can focus on us first – right?"

"Absolutely," Anna whispered, still leaning in close. Collen then brushed his lips against hers, just as deliberately as she had done before, before pulling her in for a deep kiss. Every part of her body responded with an instant flash of heat. Feeling his warm mouth against hers still seemed impossible at times, as she wasn't entirely able to separate his very real presence in her life from the dreams that had haunted her for so long.

It had been worth it not to make a big deal about the fight with Alyssa. Some things just weren't worth losing these kinds of moments for...

"Then I guess this means we have nothing to worry about," Collen tenderly murmured in Anna's ear – and as she closed her eyes, she felt the tidal wave of goose bumps sweep over her flesh, moving along in perfect rhythm with the rushing flow of emotions constantly spiraling around her heart.

A few days later, Anna was finally on her way to meet Alyssa for lunch. Collen had already gone back to DC at this point, so she was grateful for the company. After two incredible weeks together, she had been finding it difficult to settle back into her normal every day routine. He wasn't scheduled to return for another month though, so she knew this was only the beginning.

As she pulled into the parking lot of the restaurant, she quickly looked around for her sister's car. She was feeling nervous, which seemed strange because Alyssa was the one person in her life that she had always felt comfortable around. It was probably inevitable though, considering all that had happened the past few weeks.

Anna parked and immediately jumped out of her car and headed towards the restaurant. The instant she opened the door, her sister's face was the first thing she saw.

They didn't say anything, but instead ran towards each other and ended up in a huge hug.

"I missed you!" Anna exclaimed.

"I missed you too!" Alyssa happily replied.

It didn't take long for the hostess to sit them at a table, and before Anna could even think about being nervous anymore, both of them were talking non-stop.

Alyssa told Anna all about their parents and how good it had been to be home. Their dad was spending a lot of time fixing up the house. He wasn't at all qualified to make home repairs though, so most of the time his attempts were followed up with a visit from their cousin, who had his own contracting business. As for their mom…well, she accused Alyssa of being too skinny, which all good moms do. So, she cooked for her constantly.

"I seriously think I gained ten pounds!" Alyssa said as she wrapped her arms around her stomach to try and hide what could only be invisible flab.

"You look great though!" Anna replied honestly. "I'm

already jealous thinking of all the awesome food you got to eat! I need to go home and visit soon. It's just been too easy to let work and everything else get in the way."

They both knew what "everything else" was code for, but neither sister decided to elaborate.

"Yeah," Alyssa said with a smile on her face. "Going home always helps." She then grabbed a menu and started pretending to read the daily specials.

"So…" Anna teasingly said. "How are you feeling? It seems like you're doing better, but I want to talk about anything that's on your mind."

Alyssa put the menu down and sighed before finally responding.

"You're not going to like it."

Anna hated when people started conversations that way.

"Just spill it," Anna quickly spat out. She figured her sister was ready to give her a heart-to-heart about Collen, but she promised herself that she wouldn't get defensive. So, she braced herself for what was coming.

Unfortunately, she had braced herself for the wrong thing.

"I'm moving."

"What?!?!" Anna practically shouted, as several people sitting at the tables around them turned in her direction. "How can you be moving?!?!"

Anna watched as Alyssa sat up and then began fidgeting with her silverware. Eventually, she pushed the entire set aside and looked away.

"I can't stay here Anna. It's not working."

"What do you mean it's not working? You're in school…you have a good job…you have me…you have friends…what else do you need?"

"Don't you see?" Alyssa said desperately. "None of those things are working. I've been in school forever and I still don't know what I want to do. I pretty much lost my job when I took off to see mom and dad, and…"

"Wait," Anna said in a stern voice. "You didn't tell your boss you needed time off? You just left? Why would you do that?"

"No," Alyssa smartly responded. "I actually did ask him. He just said no."

"And you still went?!?!"

"Of course I still went! I had to get out of here! I had to think!"

"But Alyssa! Don't you see? If you just pick up and…"

"Anna! Stop it! You're missing the point!" Alyssa interrupted. "Don't get crazy about this! This isn't about work. It's about me. I'm lost! Me! I don't know what I'm doing! Jess was the only thing I was sure about and look how that turned out! How messed up is that? Shouldn't I want more for myself? I can't keep doing this! I need to pull my shit together!"

Anna gasped as she heard the simple swear word come out of her sister's mouth. Alyssa just smirked though, as she reached for the cocktail menu, obviously needing a drink to help calm her nerves.

"Yes," she responded coolly. "I said shit. Sue me."

Several thoughts went through Anna's mind over the next couple of seconds. She realized that she could continue to press Alyssa's AWOL status at work, or she could just listen. The latter seemed like the harder of the two choices, which is what made Anna realize it was the right thing to do. As much as she wanted her sister to see things the same way she did, the reality was that they were two different people. If Alyssa was finally trying to make a path for herself, Anna knew that this was not a time for lectures…and, to be honest, hearing her finally say the dreaded "shit word" was pretty amazing.

"Yup," Anna smirked back, with a twinkle in her eye, "you've definitely been hanging out with mom." At that point, both sisters broke out in hysterical laughter. The waiter that had started to head their way after seeing Alyssa pick up the cocktail menu, quickly changed directions and shot towards another table.

"I know right?" Alyssa cried out. "She loves to say 'shit' any chance she gets!"

Anna was laughing so hard, there were tears in her eyes.

She could barely get two words out, as she reached into her purse for a tissue to wipe the moisture away before her supposed "waterproof" mascara started smearing.

It was so easy to laugh with her sister. It was moments like this that reminded her no matter how different they were, they would always be there for each other. Not because they were family either, but because they were the very best of friends – the truest of friends.

It was at that instant, even through the laughter, that Anna couldn't help but think about how much she was going to miss her.

After they had finally managed to calm down, the waiter came back and took their drink and appetizer orders. All that was left now were the details.

"So, you're really moving?" Anna asked sadly. "This isn't a joke to get me back for being such a pain in the ass?"

"Not a joke," Alyssa replied gently. "I promise. Although, that would have been a good payback attempt…" She looked at her sister and smiled.

"But, where will you go?" Anna asked, thinking of how strange it must feel to just decide to pick up and move with no real plan in place. When she moved with Collen, it was such a different experience. They had each other. They were going to start a life together. Her little sister was going to do this all alone.

Was this really the best idea?

"Well," Alyssa said, "I've actually been thinking about it a lot. At first, I considered Arizona or Colorado, but those are too close. It would be too easy to just keep coming back here to visit. I don't think I'd really allow myself to settle in somewhere new, you know?"

It made total sense to Anna, but she had suddenly lost the ability to speak as the reality of her sister's decision started to work its way through her mind. So, instead of replying, she took a long drink of ice water. Alyssa didn't notice her hesitation though and kept talking.

"Then it hit me. Why not go somewhere I've never been

before? Somewhere exciting? So, I've decided on Chicago. I have a couple of friends from high school that moved out there after we graduated. I've already called them and…"

Anna quickly stopped drinking as she tried to keep from choking on her water.

"Wait! Stop. Are you serious?" Her ability to speak had come back full force. "You can't just move that far away!"

"Why not?" Alyssa responded calmly. "People do it all the time Anna. I'm not worried. It will be fine. In fact, I haven't felt this comfortable with a decision in a long time. I really do think this is the right thing to do."

Anna knew the look on her face had to be a mix of horror and confusion, but Alyssa didn't let on. So, she instantly started grasping for reasons to toss at her sister so that she would reconsider her decision.

"But, there will be so much to figure out…you'll probably have to rent a truck to move everything…and how much will an apartment cost there? What about a job? School..?" Even as the questions fell from her mouth though, Anna could clearly see that she wasn't going to change Alyssa's mind.

"You don't have to worry about any of those things Anna. That's *my* job. Like I said, it's time for me to get my shit together." Alyssa picked up the fresh drink that the server had put down in front of her seconds before and held it up in the air. "Now, I think we should celebrate!"

Anna felt torn. She didn't want to celebrate losing her sister to this move, but she could see how content Alyssa was with her decision. Maybe this really was the start of something great for her. How could she not want to celebrate that?

So, she hesitantly reached for her glass, and in the brief moment it took to pull it towards her, she saw a quick flash of her sister's face when they were kids. She was so little, so trusting, so eager. As she looked up though, she clearly realized that there was no small girl sitting in front of her. All she could see now was a confident young woman, ready to start the next chapter of her life.

Anna had to admit, it was pretty inspiring – and she was

very proud.

She put her glass in the air next to Alyssa's and felt the smile more easily spread across her face. It felt good to be happy for her. It felt right.

Alyssa instantly smiled too, excited to see that her sister was on board.

"To Chicago!" Alyssa cried out.

Anna tilted her glass forward, feeling the infectious enthusiasm start radiating towards her.

"To Chicago," she genuinely replied, her words quickly followed by the clinking of both glasses.

As she took her drink though, she felt the cool liquid slowing trying to make its way around the lump in her throat. She forced herself to swallow everything down, as she kept her eyes locked on Alyssa's – which were shining bright with a joy illuminated even more by the possibility of a new beginning just for her alone.

It was then, at that very moment, that Anna couldn't help but wonder if she had ever wanted such a thing for herself.

CHAPTER TWENTY-FOUR

Later that night, Anna told Collen over the phone about Alyssa's plans to move. He surprised her by taking a positive approach and insisted that a change of scenery could only be a good thing. It helped Anna become a little more comfortable with the idea, but she couldn't deny that she was still somewhat worried.

She shared her concerns with Alex and Cora a couple of days later. They had met up for happy hour to celebrate a milestone for Cora. She had been promoted at work, and Alex couldn't be more excited.

"Now I have myself a real life sugar mama!" he told Anna enthusiastically. Cora instantly started laughing as she exchanged a delighted look with Anna.

"Let me tell you," Cora said as she leaned forward so that Anna could hear her better in the noisy bar. "There is nothing like having a fiancé that is supportive of your job!"

"Speaking of fiancé..." Alex replied as he glanced at Cora. "We need to finally set a date!"

"Hey buddy! Onc thing at a time!" Cora responded teasingly. "This lady has to focus on work! I can't just start slacking off now!"

"Well," he said coyly, "I just don't want us to take too

long. I need to lock you in while you're still hot and successful!" Cora gave him a look of mock horror but couldn't hold onto it long and instantly started giggling.

"We'll see," she then responded with a wide smile on her face. "I can't make you any promises though. I might have some new prospects lining up around the corner now!"

Alex instantly looked at Anna in pretend shock.

"Did you know about this?" he asked. "You were supposed to be my friend first!"

"Hey buddy!" Anna replied, mimicking Cora's tone from a few moments before. "We ladies stick together!"

"Foiled again!" Alex instantly replied while holding his fist up in the air. He then turned to Cora. "I guess I'm just going to have to make the most of this while I can!" he said happily as he raised up his beer mug and nodded to Cora.

"To you my dear," he said sweetly.

"To you too baby," Cora blissfully replied as she raised her wine glass in response.

"Oh my God!" Anna teasingly shouted at them. "You two are ridiculous! Seriously! Get married already so that you'll stop being so mushy around everybody!"

All three then broke into laughter as the energy in the room continued to vamp up around them, buzzing with the cumulative excitement of all the other happy people enjoying an evening with friends. Anna couldn't help but take a moment to soak it all in, as she gazed at a table of women dressed in business casual outfits across from them. Their clothes said one thing, while the look on their faces and exuberance in their voices definitely implied that the work day was long over.

"So?" Cora then asked as she broke Anna's concentration. "We need details about this sudden move Alyssa is making! You didn't say too much when we talked on the phone."

"Well," Anna started, "she is planning to leave in about six months."

"This summer then?" Alex responded as he tossed some beer nuts in his mouth.

"Yup," Anna said gloomily before taking a small drink of

her martini.

"Wow! That's exciting though, right?" Cora replied cheerfully, obviously trying to turn Anna's mood back around.

"Absolutely," Anna said nodding her head up and down, "but I'm not sure that she's really thought it through."

"Are you kidding me?" Alex said with a laugh. "Alyssa is one of the smartest people I know. She wouldn't just pick up and leave without thinking it through. She may be young, but she's not stupid!"

Anna gave Alex a small smile, as she let his words sink in. Perhaps she really was worrying for nothing and was unconsciously assuming Alyssa would need to turn around later and come home, just like she did.

"It's just," she started trying to explain to her friends, "I keep thinking about when I moved. I thought I had it all figured out too, and look what happened. I don't want that to happen to her. I don't want her to be faced with disappointment again. She's already been through enough with Jess."

"But Anna," Cora replied, "this is different. Alyssa isn't moving with someone. She's moving for herself."

For herself. The words had a strange effect on Anna, suddenly making her feel very inexperienced. She nervously glanced down at the table, unable to look her friends straight in the eye.

"I guess I'm probably not the right person to be giving her advice about moving, huh?" Anna sadly responded, as she realized that her point of view may be tainted.

"Oh, no! That's not true at all!" Cora quickly shot back. She reached out and took Anna's hands in hers, as both friends made eye contact again. "What I meant was that you moved for a very different reason – to start a future with Collen. Alyssa is moving to start a future too, but on her own terms with no one to derail her, except herself. It doesn't make your experience any less important though Anna. It just means that the outcomes don't have to be the same. Does that make sense?"

Cora looked anxious as she waited for Anna to reply. She didn't need to worry though. Anna knew she was right, just like Alex was right. Her sister's move was an entirely different situation.

"It makes total sense," Anna finally said, "and I really appreciate you talking to me about this you guys. I'm sorry if I'm being a total downer. It's just a lot to take in, you know? It's a lot of change all at once." She looked down at her martini to take another drink and realized it was almost gone. Obviously, the reality of her sister's move was turning her into a drunk. She pushed the glass away and regrettably reached for her water, instantly thinking to herself how much better the martini had tasted after she took a long drink.

"Speaking of that," Alex slowly started, "how are things with Collen?"

Anna had been wondering if her friends would feel comfortable enough to bring Collen up. Suddenly, she was thinking one more drink might be a good idea after all.

"Honestly?" Anna asked carefully. "We're wonderful. *He's* wonderful. I know this is going to sound bad to you, but it's as though everything in DC never happened. I feel like we're in a stronger place than we ever were. Maybe it's just because we've missed each other so much? So, we're both focused on each other in a way we never did before?"

"That could be it," Cora replied, giving Alex a quick look. Anna could see she was holding back.

"Cora, you don't have to hide your feelings. I totally understand if you're still worried. A lot happened and I know that you want me to stay level-headed about all of this."

"Which is pretty impossible to do," Alex finally chimed in.

"What do you mean?" Anna asked with a confused look on her face.

"Anna, there is no way you can't be totally caught up in him again. He was everything to you. I know how much you loved him. I can't even imagine what it must feel like to lose that." Alex unconsciously reached out and took Cora's hand in his. "And then to have him actually come back to you years later? It must seem like a gift, rather than a test."

"A test?" Anna was genuinely lost at this point.

"Maybe that's the wrong way to phrase it," Alex slowly said, as he looked down at the table in thought. "What I'm trying to say is that just because Collen's back, it doesn't have to mean what you think it must mean. It doesn't have to be a second chance."

"But, that's exactly what it is Alex," Anna instantly replied with a serious look in her eyes. "I don't see how it can be anything else. He's told me that he still loves me. We are so connected emotionally, that I can't even describe it in words. It's amazing! It's everything I always wanted for us!"

"Anna," Cora replied carefully. "Do you think you're connected because you both are truly in the same place, or do you think it's because it just feels good to be together again? Have you even talked about what happened? Or been honest about the relationships you've had since then?"

Anna didn't like where this was going, as she knew what Cora was trying to do. So, she stayed quiet long enough for her friend to finish saying what was on her mind.

"I'm just worried that if you don't get to the root of why things went wrong the first time, how do you know he won't do the same thing again? How can you really know that he actually does want more this time?"

There it was. The question that Anna had tried to ask that first night her and Collen were back together, but that had never really been answered. She took a few moments to think about how to respond, knowing that her answer could mean a lot more than she wanted to Cora.

"All I can do is trust him," Anna finally replied. "And I really do Cora. I trust him completely and I know that he won't walk away from us again. That probably sounds crazy, but I don't see how I can have all of this love for someone if we weren't meant to be together. That just seems…well, it seems too cruel."

The three friends were then quiet for a few seconds, as Anna's words sunk in and they tried to push aside unspoken worries.

Anna knew that life wasn't a fairy tale and that there were no guarantees, but she still couldn't help but believe in fate and moments that were "meant to be". If there were no second chances, then how could anything good ever happen to the people that had made mistakes…that had gone down the wrong path…that had broken someone's heart?

"You're right," Cora finally said with a kind smile on her face. "That would be too cruel. I know that someone like you deserves something wonderful. So, if this is it, then I can't wait to see how it all turns out. I can't wait to be able to share in your amazing happiness."

Cora's eyes were shining bright, as Anna got up from the table and walked towards her. She felt the rush of emotions as they hugged and then looked at Alex standing behind them.

"Geez Anna…you sure know how to make everything so dramatic," he said in a teasing voice as he put his hand on her right shoulder and squeezed.

"I know," Anna replied as she stepped back from Cora and looked at both of her friends. "I know," she repeated again and sighed. She then reached up to her face, and quickly wiped away the warm, wet tears.

"You see what I mean?" Alex then shouted out as he threw his arms in the air. "Drama, drama, drama! Have we all forgotten something here? This is supposed to be a celebration! Let's get another round! The night is young!" He then grabbed Cora and twirled her around in an awkward dance move.

"The night is young?" Cora said as she giggled. "You know that totally makes you sound super old, right?"

"Yes ma'am!" Alex replied as he put Cora into a dangerously looking dip move. He then placed her gently in a chair and gave her a quick kiss on the forehead, before taking the last drink of his beer.

Alex was obviously done talking about Collen, but Anna didn't mind. This latest conversation had been a big step for all of them. She watched as he walked towards the bar to grab another round of drinks. She was definitely feeling a lot better than before when it came to Alyssa's move, but now she had another nagging thought in the forefront of her mind — and Cora had been the one who put it there.

It was true that she and Collen were doing wonderful, but it was also true that he had made it clear he didn't want to focus on the past — or even the future for that matter. Their conversation that first night at the hotel when Anna had finally spoken up had potential, but they didn't get very far. So, as much as Anna loved where they were at now, she knew that it couldn't be enough…and for the first time, if she was really going to be honest with herself, she knew that it shouldn't be.

♪♪♪♪

so, i'll put you in a song and sing you,

in a dream and dream you,

in a wish…believe you

— RAY ORTIZ,
"Waiting for You"

CHAPTER TWENTY-FIVE

Collen was finally back in town for work, but Anna was struggling to get herself ready to meet him at his hotel. She had been fighting a horrible cold for about a week and it had definitely taken its toll. It seemed to her as though the body aches were getting worse, and she felt as though she had a tissue constantly stuck to her face as she struggled with a runny nose and cough. Collen knew she was sick, but she had tried to downplay it over the past couple of days, not wanting to ruin their time together.

When she finally showed up at his hotel room though, it only took Collen a quick second to realize that they were not going out to dinner.

"Baby! You look awful! Why didn't you tell me you were this sick?" He quickly ushered Anna through the door and led her to a small sofa. As she sat there, feeling the body aches start to fully take over, she couldn't help but notice how nice the room was, when he had in fact stayed here the last time. Obviously, she hadn't taken the time to check out the décor during that previous visit though.

"I'm sorry," Anna said in a sad, soft voice before going into a coughing fit. "I honestly thought I'd be better by now, but I feel like it's getting worse!"

"Well, it's a good thing I'm here to take care of you then – right?"

"But what if you get sick?" Anna sweetly asked. She knew that she should have thought about that before showing up at his door, but the idea of seeing him was all that had mattered at the time.

"Don't worry. I won't get sick. I never do," Collen said this not in a reassuring manner, to help squash her concerns, but more as an explanation of simple fact.

Anna thought back for a few seconds then and quickly realized that he was right. She hadn't seen him sick once when they were in school, or even while they lived in DC. It obviously wasn't something that she had noticed before, but now it was just another trait that made him special when compared to everyone else…at least to her.

She smiled up at him dreamily, loving that if she had to be sick, at least it was here – with him. Collen responded, not with a smile, but instead with a smirk.

"Hmmm…" he started slowly, "has someone had a little too much cold medicine?"

"Nope," Anna replied softly, as she began to lay herself down on the sofa. "I haven't had any. It's bad to drive when you're medicated."

"It's also bad to drive when you're sick," Collen said in a teasing, but stern voice.

"I'm sorry…I just wanted to see you so bad. I missed you."

Collen was now helping Anna up from the sofa, and she felt a flush of heat rush through her body. For once though, it wasn't from his touch. She definitely had a fever. As the realization hit, she felt herself start to swerve slightly and instinctively leaned into him.

He smelled so good. She couldn't place the name of the scent exactly, but it was one she definitely remembered from their past together. A flurry of memories from that time started to emerge, but suddenly dissolved away, as the virus cruelly moved through her body – insistent on ruining their night together.

"Okay. I think you need some rest," Collen said in a soothing voice as he felt Anna's body temperature heat up. "Let's get you in bed. I'll order us some room service and we can put on a movie. No night on the town for you."

By then, they had reached the other side of his large, elegant hotel room and Anna had to admit that the sound of food she didn't have to cook herself, along with a king-sized bed, was exactly what she needed. In fact, she actually couldn't help but be grateful that she had gotten sick while Collen was in town. Any other time, she would have been a slave to her old, lumpy living room couch, with nothing to comfort her but reruns of cheesy television shows from the 80's and an unappetizing can of soup.

Yes. She was lucky to have him.

As she lay underneath the fluffy, soft down comforter, she heard him pick up the phone and start talking to the room service attendant. Only the first couple of sentences floated through her mind though, as the overwhelming lethargy that comes from sickness took over, and she fell into a deep sleep.

The thing about a deep sleep is that it is often accompanied by long, eventful dreams. As Anna wandered through scenes full of shadows and fuzzy images that were engulfing, and much less comforting than she would have liked, she felt a familiar wave of anxiety start to fill her with fear. It was that type of feeling that morphs and grows with every new landscape and turn of the story speeding through her exhausted mind...the type that never allows for a restful sleep, no matter how much it's needed or desired. The type that takes over completely and stays long after the dreamer has woken.

Unfortunately, for Anna, it hit even harder once her eyes finally opened and she rolled over in bed to reach out for Collen – only to find him gone. She instantly shot up into a seated position and looked around the quiet room, but she didn't see him anywhere. The bathroom door was open and the light was off. The television was on, but muted and tuned to an infomercial that appeared to be selling the latest and greatest unnecessary kitchen appliance.

Her head then turned towards the desk in the corner and she felt a wave of relief hit as her gaze fell on Collen's jacket, still hanging over the leather-bound office chair. He hadn't left after all. The past few weeks had been real. The dreamful sleep just a result of a high fever, an empty stomach, and an achy body.

Anna felt embarrassment start to take over as she realized how bad she had overreacted. Of course Collen hadn't "left her". She was in his hotel room for crying out loud! They were back together!

As she continued to internally scold herself for being so lame, she slowly got up from the bed. Although it hadn't been dreamless, the sleep had helped a little and she didn't feel as sluggish as before. She started walking towards the bathroom then, still wondering where Collen could have gone, when she suddenly heard the faint sound of his laughter in the hallway.

There was no fighting if off this time. The anxiety was definitely back.

"Why was he in the hallway? Who could he be talking to? What time was it anyway?"

The questions continued to drown her every thought as she turned to look at the clock on the bedside table and saw it was a little past midnight. She had slept for almost five hours. The realization made her look around the room and take in what she had missed during her frantic search for Collen. Her eyes landed on the room service tray in the small living area, one plate empty and covered with a cloth napkin, a bowl covered with plastic wrap off to the side. It had to be her soup, obviously untouched due to her body's desire for sleep rather than food.

Anna couldn't believe she had slept the evening away. Collen wasn't even going to be in town that long – only a week this time.

"What was I thinking?" she said aloud to herself, the

frustration obvious in her voice. She started towards the door to the room so that she could apologize to Collen for wasting his first night back, when she heard him laugh again.

She knew that laugh. She hadn't caught it the first time, but she heard it clear as day now.

It was the way he laughed, not necessarily when he was flirting, but when he was intrigued by the conversation – or more so, when he was engrossed in someone. He used to do it with her a lot when they first started dating, and she had loved it. Over time though, as with most relationships, those kinds of special gestures change over into something more normal…regular…common. It honestly wasn't until a couple of years later that Anna noticed she didn't hear it anymore. It had taken hearing his laughter from across the room during a night out in DC for her to finally realize it, having mistakenly been distracted by what she thought had been their secure relationship. He hadn't been talking to just anyone the night it happened either.

He had been talking to "her".

The anxiety was now replaced by something else…something worse…something ugly.

Jealousy. Distrust. Suspicion.

Yes. It was very obvious now.

Collen was definitely talking to a woman.

CHAPTER TWENTY-SIX

During the three weeks that Anna had tried to salvage her relationship with Collen all those years ago, she spent every day constantly worrying and fixated on his every movement. If she called and he didn't answer, she instantly thought he must be with someone else and was avoiding her. So, when he would finally come home after work, she found herself watching him, waiting for some sort of tell-tale sign about what he had done all day…who had he talked to, ate lunch with, sat next to on the train…the fear that he had done something with someone else, anyone else, would cruelly attach itself to her every thought. All of the little things that made up the hours of his day, the ones that she had never before given a second thought about, now she couldn't push out of her mind – and Anna knew why.

It was because those little things that she had chosen to ignore…the incidents that seemed like nothing when compared to three years of happiness…they should have allowed her to see the truth. A truth that would have exposed itself to her long before Collen had, and perhaps, even less callously.

There had been so many of those moments too. He had practically tossed them around like poorly hidden Easter eggs for her to find. She hated herself now for missing them...for being so stupid and blind...for trusting him so much. When she looked back on the little things, one by one, they didn't seem like much. It wasn't until she piled them, one on top of the other, that she realized how obvious his transgressions had been.

There were the late night text messages that he claimed came from work due to the need for someone to "touch base". He was an intern after all and had to prove he was committed. Of course, there was happy hour every week too. Collen had told her that no one's significant others attended because it was important for the team to bond outside of the office. So, she had never questioned it. As with most indiscretions in a relationship, there were also plenty of missed dinners followed up with vague explanations that she told herself were simply a side-effect of working so hard.

There had been much more though...

The casual glances at other women when they were out, or how he went out of this way to be much nicer than necessary to an attractive waitress or bartender. There had even been a couple of times when Anna felt somewhat invisible as he allowed himself to become engrained in a conversation with another woman when they were at an event or a party. During those occasions, she had walked away after the first few minutes had passed, wondering how he could be so inconsiderate. He always had an excuse though, like he had simply been networking or was just trying to be nice. He would then put his arms around her and tell her that she shouldn't feel left out. She was making too much of things and should just let it go. She was being emotional for no reason.

Collen would never apologize for his behavior though. Not ever.

Even on the night she heard the long-missed sound of his laughter, he tossed her complaints aside, and for the first time, he got angry when she shared her concerns. They fought the entire way home, but he wouldn't give her the satisfaction of admitting he had been flirting. He said he didn't flirt with co-workers and admonished her for trying to make him sound so unprofessional. He told her that if he had been flirting, then why in the hell would he have introduced her? Did she really think he was that stupid? After a while, he completely refused to talk about it anymore and insisted on sleeping in the guest room once they got home.

It had been one of the worst fights they had ever had. Anna had never seen Collen so furious and could only think it was because she actually had offended him. All night long she lay in bed thinking about what had happened, and by the time the first delicate rays of sunlight were quietly pouring into the guest room window, she had woken him up with a soft kiss. She apologized for being so selfish and for not listening to him. She told him that she had no right to react that way, and she begged him not to think of her as an envious, suspicious woman.

She promised it would never, ever happen again…and it didn't.

Because even during those last three weeks when Anna knew with her whole heart that he couldn't be trusted, and even when she finally did put all of the pieces together after they broke up, she refused to let that side of herself come out.

It wasn't because she thought being non-reactive would be a demonstration of strength though. If she had to be honest with herself, she knew it was because she was afraid to drive him away even faster – and that she just couldn't bear.

So, even with all of the evidence in front of her at the end, Anna looked the other way. Because even moments with him encircled by shadows and doubt were, for her, far better than losing him completely…and at the time, she thought her unquestioning behavior would be proof that he should stay.

At the time, it was the best she could do.

Tonight though, as she stood on the other side of the hotel room door, she realized that now it was time to do better.

CHAPTER TWENTY-SEVEN

As Collen quietly opened the hotel room door, Anna instantly felt her whole body tense up. Her head felt heavy from both the sickness and the flood of memories that had been tearing through her mind, but she knew she had to push past everything if she was going to take control of the moment.

"Who were you talking to?" she asked coolly as Collen quickly turned his head towards her, the look of surprise clearly evident on his face.

"Baby! Why are you up? You should be resting." He rushed over and started to turn her towards the direction of the bed, the action almost metaphorical as he so obviously ignored her question and tried to divert her. Before she knew she was going to do it, Anna instantly removed his hands from her shoulders and flung herself back around.

Not this time.

"Collen," her voice was trembling more than she liked, but she didn't care. "I woke up and you were gone. But, I could clearly hear you talking in the hallway, and so now I'm wondering who the hell would be calling you this late at night?" She could feel her face turning crimson as the anger took full control and she felt every part of her body start to shake. She quickly crossed her arms across her chest in an attempt to maintain a firm stance.

"You're kidding me, right?" Collen responded nastily, his voice no longer dripping with mock concern. It was shocking how quickly his mood had changed, but not to her. She had seen this happen before, and now she knew what triggered it. He didn't like feeling cornered. He wasn't used to being caught. "You seriously better be messing with me right now Anna. I'm not in the mood for this."

"You're not in the mood? I'm the one who's sick Collen! You think this is fun for me? I didn't come over here to wake up to my boyfriend hiding out in the hallway talking to god knows who in the middle of the night!"

"You need to stop," Collen firmly and bitterly snapped back. "Don't do this Anna. This isn't the place or the time."

"What are you fucking talking about? The place or the time? Why are you making it sound like I'm the one acting inappropriately here? You are the one who is avoiding the question. So, I'll ask you ONE MORE TIME. Who were you talking to?"

Anna watched as a wave of emotion swept across Collen's face. She couldn't tell if it was good or bad, as he suddenly looked down at the floor. She could sense in his body language that he was trying to compose himself. What had only been seconds, suddenly felt like hours as the anticipation of his response weighed her down even more. She felt a strong desire to step backwards and sit on the edge of the bed, but she couldn't move…couldn't think…couldn't breathe. Everything stopped as she waited for him to finally say something.

When Collen eventually raised his head, he firmly locked his eyes on hers. There was no more doubt. Now Anna knew for sure something was wrong, and sadly, she knew she wasn't ready for what was about to happen.

As Collen spoke, she felt a physical reaction instantly begin to take over her body while his words tumbled around in her mind.

What had he said??? There is no way he said that name. No…no…no…no…

Her thoughts were in a tailspin now and Anna could no longer focus on the rest of what Collen was saying, his voice now distant and foggy. Blackness began to creep into her line of sight and she felt an intense heaviness start to firmly, ruthlessly pull at her until Anna slowly began to understand what was going to happen.

Luckily, Collen must have seen it too, because the last thing she remembered was him reaching out towards her as she fell towards the floor into a dark sea – one that she could only hope would momentarily free her from the reality of long lost love and insurmountable regrets.

Anna had only blacked out once before in her life. It had been on a trip to Mexico with her family when she was in high school. It was their first big vacation, and after proving her and Alyssa could behave responsibly, their parents had left them to enjoy the beach so that they could go shopping and enjoy cocktails away from the prying eyes of children.

Both sisters couldn't have been happier to be unsupervised for a few hours and they made sure to make the most of their time out in the extra, large swimming pool under a bright, hot sun. The problem was, that without their mother around to make sure they were staying hydrated, it had been too easy for them to forget that high temperatures could take their toll.

Anna had been the one to learn that lesson in the most excruciating way, when she passed out as they were walking back to the room. One minute she was fine, and the next, she was on the scorching ground. She had never passed out before, so she didn't know what was coming when she felt the unnatural wave of nausea and warmth begin to wash over her. Fortunately though, for her and Alyssa, a couple of workers from the resort were walking behind them when it happened. They were able to quickly move Anna to a lounge chair under an umbrella and call for a medical attendant using a walkie-talkie.

A few seconds later, Anna awoke to a horribly skinned knee that would leave a scar for the rest of her life and a crowd of curious vacationers looking down upon her as she lay on a bright, blue lounge chair. Alyssa was crying hysterically too, as she had never seen anyone pass out before and thought her sister's instant, dramatic plunge to the ground meant she had died.

It didn't take long for the resort to locate her parents, and so thirty minutes and two bottles of water later, Anna was tucked in her bed back in the hotel room. She had never felt so tired in her life. It was as if every cell in her body had been turned off and each one was now slowly coming back on – one by one…like dusty lightbulbs in an old, empty house. She slept for hours and didn't get up until late the next morning, only to spend the rest of the vacation hiding in the shade or hurrying to the bathroom since she was drinking water non-stop.

Anna never went to a beach resort again. It had lost its appeal after that and she still couldn't help but look at the scar on her knee and feel her cheeks flush. Some things a person just can't ever shake off.

Humiliation was like that.

So was love…

CHAPTER TWENTY-EIGHT

"Anna...Anna...can you hear me? Anna? Are you okay? Anna?"

Anna awoke from this latest incident in a much different position than she had been in all those years ago. The ground was carpeted and soft, and somehow, a pillow had been placed under her head. This time, there were no gawking strangers surrounding her, emanating with nervousness and pity while murmuring amongst themselves. Instead, her name was being gently whispered over and over, as her hair was brushed away from the sides of her face, and her body was cradled within strong, familiar arms.

She was not a young girl either. This time, she was a grown woman...and most importantly, she had been caught before she hit the ground.

Or had she?

"Anna? Anna?" Collen's voice was clearly coming through, even though Anna could feel the fog hadn't lifted entirely. It was this realization – this feeling of a crushing, cloudy reality – that harshly reminded her of what had happened over the past few minutes. So, even though her arms felt like heavy, foreign instruments, she used all of the strength she had to push him away.

"Don't…" she slowly replied, as she felt him instinctively try and wrap her up closer to him. Maybe he thought she was confused, or perhaps even scared, but Anna was far from it.

"No! Don't! Don't!" Anna began to shout back as she awkwardly tried to sit up on her own and move Collen away from her at the same time. "Stop it! Don't touch me!"

"Anna!" Collen yelled back. "What's wrong with you? You're acting insane! You just passed out! Let me help you!" He reached out for her right hand but she instantly pulled it away, the anger now supplying her tired muscles with adrenaline.

"No! I can do it myself! I'm fine!"

"You are definitely not fine! You're sick and dehydrated! You probably need a doctor!"

"No I don't! I'm fine! I'm fine! Just get away from me! I don't need a doctor! I don't need you! I don't need anybody!"

Anna knew as the words spilled out of her mouth that none of them were true, but there was no hope now. She had to continue down this fiery path and finally try to get answers for all of the questions that had quietly, yet quickly, continued to build roadblocks between them.

"Anna," Collen replied in an annoyed voice. "I don't get it. What's wrong? Where is this coming from?"

She couldn't help but roll her eyes like a teenager.

"Whatever Collen," Anna sarcastically shot back. She slowly walked over to the sofa she had sat on a few brief hours before, stopping only to grab some tissue from a small, decorative table as she went by. "I may have passed out, but I don't have amnesia. I want the truth now. All of it. Why were you talking to *her*?" She was now staring straight at him, her eyes quickly filling up with tears. "I don't understand! Why would you do that? I don't understand…I don't understand…"

It was no use. Regardless of how strong she wanted to be,

Anna then felt everything inside her begin to crumple up, as the cumulative effects of the evening took her to another emotional breaking point.

As if passing out hadn't been bad enough. Now she couldn't stop crying. It was infuriating to be so weak.

"Anna!" Collen quickly swooped down and sat next to her on the sofa. "You are making way too much of this! I promise! It's not what you think. She is interviewing for a new job tomorrow and called to ask me for some advice."

"At midnight?!"

"Yes! I know! It seems weird, but she was nervous and couldn't sleep. I was just trying to be nice." His hand was now softly resting on her right thigh, and Anna felt something inside twist and turn as she tried to distance herself from his touch. In an attempt to remain focused and not let her emotions take over any more than they already had, she slowly stood up and walked a few feet away so that she could lean against the wall. The tears were fierce and streaming down her face now, but she barely felt them. In fact, the more the hurt poured in, the more she began to feel numb.

"So, you both are still pretty close then, huh? If she calls you when she can't sleep?" Anna's head was pounding now, as she allowed herself to absorb this new information. Her eyes were on the plush carpeted floor, as she was too nervous to look at him…to hear what he would say next, but she knew there was still one more very important question to ask. She also knew that Collen wasn't going to like it.

"When were you going to tell me that you were still in touch with her?"

Collen sighed loudly and shook his head from side to side. He was still sitting on the sofa, now fully aware of her desire to be away from him. "I swear, I never intended for you to find out this way."

There was no escaping that truth. He had in fact kept it a secret. Even after all these years, it seemed neither one of them had learned a damn thing. He was still lying and she was still trying to believe in him.

Anna winced as he finished his sentence. "When you say it like that, it definitely sounds like you were hiding it from me on purpose."

"I wasn't though! I promise! We haven't talked in months!"

"Months?" Anna's face was now blank, the ability to show any sorrow now masked by total, complete confusion. "Does that mean you stayed with her long...after me, I mean? After I left?" Anna was now wishing they could go back to their rule about avoiding the past, but it was too late for that she sadly thought to herself, and she felt her knees get weaker from the cruel circumstances that had been forced upon her.

Then again, maybe they hadn't been forced, but instead had been invited in, due to her inability to stay away from this man that she loved so very much.

"Anna – please listen to me," Collen now said fervently. "None of that matters. All that matters is that I'm here with you. Why can't you see that?"

She felt the familiar tug on her heart as his words tried to burrow their way inside. She closed her eyes, but could still picture him in front of her – waiting, watching, wondering what she would do next. The uncertainty must have made him feel vulnerable, because he then said something she never expected.

"We were engaged Anna. There's the truth. Okay? We were engaged."

Everything stopped for her in that moment – or so she thought. Collen had one more surprise for her.

"I called it off though. I called it off because it never seemed right! I had never been able to stop thinking about you." He slowly walked over and took her hands in his. "So, you see? I left her...and now I choose you. That should be all that matters now. Right?"

Anna opened her eyes and looked at the man she had loved for most of her adult life.

Everything really did happen for a reason.

CHAPTER TWENTY-NINE

It had to be the most gorgeous night Anna had seen in a long time. The stars were so bright, it seemed as though they were illuminating everything around her, and a dazzling moon hung large and high in the midnight blue sky. She reached out to gently grasp the arm of a familiar face as she walked passed each group of friends, several of them with a glass of champagne in hand – eager to celebrate. The air was filled with excitement, hope, love...it couldn't help but touch the heart of everyone that had gathered together on this special, long awaited occasion.

Anna stopped a few feet away from where the band was playing and turned around so that she could take in the whole scene. She couldn't help but feel both humble and blessed to be there. When she thought of everything it had taken to finally get to this place...to finally, truly be happy...well, it seemed like a real life miracle.

She brought a fresh glass of champagne to her lips and felt the bubbly, delicious liquid slowly flow into her mouth. If champagne could taste like a romantic evening, this one was definitely a contender. She used her other hand to straighten the lines in her long, satin dress. It was the perfect length to where it barely kissed the ground as she walked. It made her feel beautiful and new…something she was also grateful for at this time in her life.

Then, as Anna looked up at the view above, she felt a strong, yet gentle hand on her shoulder. She didn't even need to turn around to know his all too familiar touch. It was as much a part of her as the joy that now lived in her heart.

She closed her eyes and felt his fingers linger on her back as he slowly moved around to face her. She took a deep breath and felt the emotions swirl up and softly begin to dance in her throat. It amazed her how much he could affect her, even after all this time.

When she finally moved her head towards him and opened her eyes, she wasn't surprised to see a brilliant shade of blue staring back down at her.

Nothing was the same after Collen had told Anna that he had chosen her over getting married. Not only did she now know the extent of the relationship that had helped trample hers into the ground, but she saw a truth that went beyond broken promises and hidden secrets. As he sat in front her and tried once again to brush everything away, she finally saw him for what he was – and she knew that if she didn't take hold of the moment, her feelings for him would be her downfall.

It was then, as he stared at her with remorseful brown eyes, when the anger finally came.

"How dare you try and make me the reason why you were too chicken shit to get married!" Anna screamed. "That is totally on you! It has nothing to do with me! How could it? You sure didn't seem to worry about me when you started cheating in the first place! And stop saying that nothing else matters! Because it does matter! It all matters! It's all connected! Don't you see that?" Her voice was breaking under the weight of everything that had happened, but it wasn't enough to make her stop. It felt too good to finally feel something other than desperate and all-consuming love for him.

"Collen, for once you need to think about what this

revelation means for me! This is a person that I have tried to avoid thinking about for years! Do you know how many times I compared myself to her? Do you know how many times I thought back on how she looked? How she talked? How she moved? I did everything I could to figure out why she would have been so important, so special, that you would leave me! And when I couldn't do that, when I couldn't bear one more moment to carry her with me, I had to try and forget everything about her! Everything about us! But, I couldn't! It was impossible! So, instead, I pushed it all as far away as I could! You…her…our life in DC…everything I thought was supposed to be my future and that was taken away – I pushed it all away just so that it could come back and clobber me tonight! So, you see! It does matter Collen! All of it matters! And just because you don't want it to, doesn't mean I'm going to shut up about it!"

"God damn it!" Collen was now shouting too. "Why can't you just let all of that go already? I've already apologized to you! I've already said I'm sorry! What is it going to take? Are you trying to torture me? Is this why you let me back in? Just to punish me? Don't you know that every time I think back on what happened between us I feel like a total piece of shit?!?!"

"Well you should feel that way!" Anna spit violently back at him. "I'm actually glad you feel that way! Because, you know what? You actually were a total piece of shit! I loved you and you took advantage of that! You took advantage of my trust! You left me feeling like nothing! And I know it's not all your fault and that I had a part to play too, but I had never wanted anything more in my life than for us to be together! I believed in you! I believed in us! How could you lie to me? Why are you still lying to me?"

"I already told you that I'm not lying! I haven't talked to her in months!"

"You were engaged!!!"

"So what?!?! Yes! We were engaged! But we aren't any more, so who fucking cares? Why do I have to tell you about something that happened after we broke up? I don't want to talk about it – okay? That doesn't make it a lie! It just means I'm over it! So you should be too!"

"Oh, yeah? Well, you know what Collen? Choosing not to tell someone something, just because you're too afraid of what it will mean, can be seen by some people – including me – as a lie. And you know why? Because you let me believe she was out of your life!"

"Well, apparently our definitions of lying are different, and it's not my fault that you made a wrong assumption. I told you that I didn't want to talk about the past, so you went and made up ideas in your head as to what that meant. That's on you! It's also obvious that you are never going to forgive me for leaving you the first time. So, now you know what Anna? I'm done! I'm not talking about this anymore!" Collen threw his hands up in the air and walked towards the office chair to grab his jacket.

"What?" Anna could feel frustration growing within her, as she watched him forcefully pull on his jacket and reach for his keys. "You're leaving? Are you seriously leaving? For the first time in weeks we're finally being real with each other and you're going to walk away?"

"Yes! I'm leaving! I'm not going to fight with you! I'm not going to fight about something that happened three years ago!"

"But it didn't happen three years ago Collen! It happened now! It happened tonight!"

Collen was already at the hotel room door, but turned around abruptly to throw the final blow.

"You know, I didn't ask for any of this! I didn't ask for her to call me! And I sure as hell didn't ask for you to treat me like some sort of asshole! I can't control people Anna! All I can do is try and love you! But right now, that seems impossible!"

As the door slammed firmly behind him, Anna felt the room start to spin around her. She quickly sat on the floor and tried to focus every thought on not blacking out again, until she realized that wasn't what was happening. For the first time since she had met Collen, she wasn't going into submissive mode, and suddenly she felt something inside her grow stronger with each passing second.

She thought about what he had said – that she made it impossible for him to love her – and she finally saw the manipulation for what it was…how easily he could turn things on her so that he wouldn't have to take any responsibility for what he had done. He had even taken that route when they first broke up, by making her feel guilty for wanting to forgive him…by implying that it was wrong and made her weak and unlovable, as though that alone was why their relationship couldn't work.

It had never been about her. She saw that now.

After a few minutes, Anna carefully got up and walked over to her cold bowl of soup. She slowly took off the plastic wrap and swallowed a small spoonful. That was all it took for her sick, tired body to want more.

So she ate. She didn't cry. She didn't pace the room. She didn't think. She just ate.

Bite by bite, she felt it continue to grow…something she hadn't known in a very long time. Something that had always been there, but had been hidden away under doubts, and fears, and distractions…something that she was sure she wouldn't lose sight of again.

Courage.

CHAPTER THIRTY

"Luke!" Anna said with a huge smile on her face. "I can't believe you're here! Thank you so much for coming!" She quickly set her glass down and laughed as he pulled her into a soft bear hug. It had been a long time, and so much had happened, but all she cared about in that moment was that her friend was home.

"How long are you in town?" Anna happily asked.

"Just a few days," Luke cheerfully replied. "I'm hoping to make the most of my time here though. It's been so long since I've seen everybody!"

"Well," Anna started in a sincere voice, "I know that it means the world to Alex and Cora that you came. They are so excited to see you!"

"I'm excited to see them!" Luke quickly responded. "I feel bad that I missed the ceremony, but my plane got delayed. How did it go?"

"Oh..." Anna said dreamily, "It was perfect Luke. Beautiful and perfect. Just like them."

"I have to say that I'm not surprised," Luke said sweetly. "I wouldn't expect anything less from those two sappy love birds!" As he finished his sentence, Anna couldn't help but laugh. She definitely didn't know anyone sappier and more in love than Alex and Cora, but it didn't make her sad anymore. It made her truly happy to know that kind of love really did exist.

"So, I heard the big news!" Luke said in an excited voice. "Is it true? Are you really moving to Chicago?"

"It's true!" Anna exclaimed as she threw her arms up in the air. "I'm going in three weeks! Alyssa had only been there a couple of months when she started hounding me to move too. At first, I thought it was a crazy idea – but now…I don't know…something just seems right about it."

"Well, I think it's a great idea!" Luke started. "If I've learned anything, it's that you never know what is waiting for you in a different part of the world."

"I know! I can't wait to hear all about your adventures! You must tell me everything while you're here! We have so much catching up to do!" Anna then looked at Luke with eyes full of gratitude – the urge to say something more apparent to both of them.

"Luke, I really need to tell you something…." she started, not wanting to lose the moment. "You see…I need to tell you that I'm sorry." Anna felt the lump in her throat fully form in a brief second, but she kept going. "I know that I wasn't the best girlfriend to you. I never fully let you in, and I wasn't truly honest about my past – I know now that it was holding me back. It held us back. You didn't deserve that…you were so wonderful and kind to me. I just need you to know that I am so very grateful for every day we had together. You may not know it, but you made me a better person. You saw something in me that I didn't even know existed. You had faith in me and I see now what a gift that was."

The tears were now softly flowing down Anna's cheeks, as Luke reached out and wiped them away.

"Oh, Anna…" he started, "You don't owe me any apologies. I loved being with you and I love seeing who you are now. If I had a little piece in that, then I am the lucky one." His blue eyes were now shining with tears of their own, as he pulled her in for another hug.

After a few moments, they stepped apart and Luke gave

Anna a serious look. "Now, you better stop crying before people start thinking you drank too much champagne!" he told her in a teasing voice.

"Ohhh…" Anna said, as she chuckled and picked up her glass, thankful that he had made a joke. "Let's not kid ourselves. We both know I probably will drink too much champagne!"

"That's my girl!" Luke proudly replied. "Just save some for me! I'm off to find the bride and groom!"

"Okay," Anna said softly to herself as she watched him walk towards Alex and Cora – before long, she saw all three get entangled in a group hug, and couldn't help but laugh. As Luke pulled away and started talking enthusiastically to Alex, Cora turned and blew a kiss to Anna, who then lifted her glass and blew a kiss back.

True love really did come in so many different forms. Anna knew that now, although it had been so hard for her to see for so long. She didn't talk to Collen again the night he stormed out of the hotel room. She thought about waiting for him to come back, but decided that there really was no more left to say. He must have felt the same way, because he never called and he didn't try and see her again either. Perhaps for some people, closure is not always a reality – not because it isn't possible, but because to close a door completely and forever would mean losing sight of something precious…

For Anna, that something precious was the mistakes it had taken for her to finally find her place in this world. She knew that her love for Collen hadn't just disappeared – love doesn't do that. She liked to think that it had transformed though…into a healthier love, a stronger love, a love that she would now carry for herself.

As she watched her beautiful friends celebrate under the bright, night sky she felt her cell phone begin to vibrate in her purse.

It could only be one person.

"Hello?" Anna asked in a mischievous voice, "Who is this?"

"It's me sister!" Alyssa joyfully replied. "How's the party going?"

"It's wonderful! They honestly couldn't have picked a more perfect day to get married."

"Man! Too bad I'm missing it! Is there champagne?"

"Oh...yes...lots!"

"Nooooo!!!!"

"Don't worry," Anna laughed, "I promise we will drink champagne when I get there."

"Yay!!!" Alyssa shrieked with glee, "I can't wait for you to come! I have so many plans for us! Sometimes, I still can't believe it's real!"

"Well, believe it! I'll be there next month. So be ready!"

"I will be!"

"Okay! I better go now though, it looks like they are getting ready to cut the cake. But, I'll call you tomorrow and tell you all about the wedding!"

"Good! I'll be waiting! Talk to you then! I love you!"

"Love you too!"

As Anna hung up the phone though, she suddenly felt an overwhelming desire to call her sister back and quickly hit redial. It rang only once before Alyssa eagerly answered.

"Hey! Did you call me by accident?"

"No," Anna began, "I forgot to tell you something."

"Okay..." Alyssa said somewhat hesitantly.

"I wanted to say that I miss you and I'm really excited to be moving." Anna tenderly replied. "Thank you so much for wanting me there with you."

"Anna! Of course I want you here!" Alyssa cheerfully answered back. "You're my big sister! Just promise me one thing though..."

"Yeah?" Anna asked in a curious voice.

"Don't get lost on the way! Please!" Alyssa laughed. "I know that you're driving yourself and it's so easy for you to get turned around! Let's make sure you know the route really well before you leave, okay?"

"Oh, don't worry..." Anna warmly replied as she rested

her hand on her heart. "I know exactly where I'm going…promise."

ACKNOWLEDGMENTS

I know with my whole heart that this book would not exist if it hadn't been for the following people…

My parents, Eileen and Ramon, who brought me into this world and have loved and supported me every single second of my life…

My beautiful friends, who fill me with joy and make me strive to be a better person so that I am more worthy of them…

My dear friend and talented photographer, Chikiyo Jackson, who gave me hours of his time and expertise to give me the perfect cover photo…

My fellow "Gallupian" and an admired musician, Prudy Dimas, who graciously allowed me to quote one of his many beautiful song lyrics…

My brother Ray, who's own lyrics carry the theme throughout the book, as it was his music that first ignited something inside me so many years ago…

My brother Joel, who has constantly inspired me through his own magnificent storytelling abilities…

My sister Maria, who has believed in me and this book from the very beginning – there are no words to describe my love and admiration for you…

And my husband Heath, who is proof that everything really does happen for a reason…I will love you forever.

ABOUT THE AUTHOR

Andrina G. Aragon is a lover of life, her family, her friends, and her mistakes – as each and every one has brought her to where she is today. She lives in Aurora, Colorado with her husband and their three dogs. This is her first novel.

Made in the USA
San Bernardino, CA
15 February 2015